Maigret on the Defensive

MAIGRET ON THE DEFENSIVE

Translated from the French by Alastair Hamilton

GEORGES SIMENON

A Helen and Kurt Wolff Book

Harcourt Brace Jovanovich, Publishers

New York and London

HBJ

Requests for permission to make copies
of any part of the work should be mailed to:
Permissions, Harcourt Brace Jovanovich, Inc.,
757 Third Avenue, New York, N.Y. 10017.

Library of Congress Cataloging in Publication Data

Simenon, Georges, 1903–
Maigret on the defensive.

Translation of: Maigret se défend.
"A Helen and Kurt Wolff book."
I. Title.
PQ2637.I53M27813   1981   843'.912   81–47576
ISBN 0–15–155557–5   AACR2

Printed in the United States of America

First American edition 1981

B C D E

Maigret on the Defensive

1

"Tell me, Maigret . . ." The words didn't strike the Superintendent at the time, but he was to remember them later. Everything was familiar, the background, the faces and even the movements of the characters, so familiar that he had long ceased to notice them. It was in the Rue Popincourt, several hundred yards from the Boulevard Richard-Lenoir, at the Pardons' house, where Maigret had for years been dining once a month.

And the doctor and his wife dined at the Superintendent's once a month, too. It gave the two women a chance to have a friendly cooking contest.

As usual they had sat on after dinner. Solange, the Pardons' daughter, pregnant for the second time, an apologetically awkward nonentity, had come to stay for a few days with her parents while her husband, an engineer in the eastern district, was attending a congress in Nice.

It was June. The day had been stifling and the night

was stormy. Through the open window the moon could occasionally be seen between two black clouds, momentarily framing them in white.

According to a tradition established during their first dinner, the ladies had served the coffee and were talking quietly at the other end of the room, leaving the two men together. It was the doctor's waiting room, and outdated magazines were piled on the tables.

In actual fact one small detail was different from the other times. While Maigret filled and lit his pipe, Pardon had disappeared for a moment and returned from his office with a box of cigars.

"I won't offer you one, Maigret."

"No thanks. Do you smoke cigars these days?"

He had only seen the doctor smoke cigarettes. After a glance at his wife, Pardon muttered:

"She told me to."

"Because of the articles on lung cancer?"

"They made a strong impression on her."

"Do you believe in them?"

Pardon shrugged.

"Even if I did . . ."

He added in a whisper:

"Outside I admit that . . ."

He cheated. At home he forced himself to smoke cigars, which didn't suit him, but elsewhere he smoked cigarettes on the sly, like a schoolboy.

He was neither tall nor fat. His dark hair was turning gray and his face was lined. The evening almost always ended with an urgent call from an invalid, and Pardon had to apologize for leaving his guests.

"Tell me, Maigret . . ."

He said it hesitantly, almost shyly.

"We must be about the same age."

"I'm fifty-two."

The doctor knew it. He looked after the Superintendent and had him in his files.

"Retirement in three years' time. We're sent packing by the police force when we're fifty-five."

There was a moment of nostalgia. The two men by the window got occasional gusts of fresh air and noticed flashes of lightning in the sky without any sound of thunder. Some windows were lit up in the house opposite; shadows passed behind the curtains; an old man, leaning on his window sill, seemed to be staring at them.

"I'm forty-nine. Three years' difference counts at school but not at our age."

Maigret didn't think he would recall the details of this idle conversation. He liked Pardon. He was one of the few men with whom he liked spending the evening.

The district doctor went on, searching for his words:

"You and I have more or less the same experience of men. Many of my clients could become yours."

It was true. In the overcrowded quarter one met with all sorts—the best and the worst.

"I'd like to ask you a question . . ."

His embarrassment was obvious. They were friends, certainly, just as the two women were friends. Nevertheless they hesitated to broach certain subjects. For instance, they never spoke about religion or politics.

"In all your career," Pardon continued, "have you ever met a really wicked criminal? I mean . . ."

He was still hesitant, trying to define his thoughts.

"A conscious criminal, of course, responsible for his

deeds, acting from pure wickedness, from vice, so to speak. I don't mean child killers, say, who are nearly all uneducated, mentally underdeveloped, and bewildered in an adult world, where they take to drink."

"You mean the pure criminal, in fact."

"Pure or impure . . Let's say the complete criminal."

"In the opinion of the penal code?"

"No. In your opinion."

Maigret, his eyes narrowed, looked at his friend through the smoke of his pipe. He focused on the cigar that Pardon held clumsily, about to drop the long ash on the carpet. He smiled, and the doctor looked at the cigar, too, in slight embarrassment.

They understood each other. This business of cigarettes and cigars had haunted the district doctor and made him, maybe unconsciously, ask his question.

He was forty-nine; he had just said so. Every day, for years, he had been bending over sick people who thought of him as a savior and expected everything from him—health, life, advice, the solution to their problems.

He had saved men, women and children. He had helped others face up to reality. Every day, at a few minutes' notice, he was called upon to make decisions more irrevocable than those of a judge in court.

After reading newspaper articles, his wife had asked him to give up cigarettes, and he hadn't had the courage to hurt or worry her by refusing. So at home he forced himself to puff clumsily at a foul-tasting cigar. But once at the wheel of his car, on his way to some sick person's bedside, he lit a cigarette with the trembling hand of a culprit.

Maigret didn't answer his friend's question at once. He almost asked:

"What about you?"

It was too easy.

"If by some misfortune I had had to become a magistrate," he began hesitantly, "or if I were on the jury for some trial . . . No, I know I wouldn't take it on myself to judge another man."

"Whatever the crime?"

"It's not the crime that counts. It's what is happening, or has happened in the head of whoever commits it. . . ."

"So you've never come across a case where you would have condemned without hesitating?"

"What you call wickedness? At first sight, yes . . . In my office I've had people I could hardly resist striking —Then, on further investigation . . ."

The conversation ended because one of the women —Maigret couldn't remember which—had come up:

"Some Armagnac?"

Pardon glanced at Maigret.

"No, thank you."

"Incidentally, when did I last examine you?"

"About a year ago."

There was a clap of thunder which seemed to roll from roof to roof, but the rain that had been expected for several days didn't come.

"Let's go into my office a moment."

Solange Pardon's first-born was asleep in a crib.

"Don't worry. He sleeps like a log. But only till five in the morning, unfortunately. Let's check your blood pressure."

Maigret took off his jacket and stripped to the waist.

Pardon had adopted the serious, distant look of his profession.

"Breathe in. Deeper. Breathe through your mouth . . . Good. Lie down here and undo your belt. I suppose you haven't decided to take it easier, as I suggested?"

"Have you?"

"I know . . . I know . . . How about your diet?"

Maigret shook his head.

"Wine, beer, alcohol? Do you drink less?"

"The only thing I've achieved is to feel guilty whenever I have a glass of beer or a liqueur. Between cases I spend days drinking only a little wine with my meals. Then I go into a bar to look at the house opposite. I smell that bitter smell, and then . . ."

Like Pardon and his cigarettes. And yet they were both men!

Maigret and his wife walked home as usual.

"How did he say you were?"

"Quite well."

It was then that all the water that had accumulated over Paris during weeks of heat chose to pour down.

"Let's take shelter in a doorway."

It was all over. Maigret had dined at the Pardons' ten days ago. It was hot again. People were leaving on vacation. In his office the Superintendent worked in his shirt sleeves, the window wide open, and the Seine had the glaucous glimmer of the sea on some calm mornings.

At half past ten, as he was going through his colleagues' reports, Joseph, the old usher, knocked at the door in a way familiar to everyone in the building. He came in without waiting for an answer and put an envelope on the Superintendent's desk.

Maigret winced when he saw the engraved heading: *Chief Commissioner of Police.*

A note was enclosed:

"Superintendent Maigret is requested to be at the Chief Commissioner's office on June 28 at 11:00 A.M."

Maigret blushed as he used to do when he was told to see the headmaster at school. June 28. He automatically looked at the calendar. It was indeed Tuesday, June 28. And it was half past ten. The summons didn't come through the post but had been delivered by hand.

After over thirty years on the police force and ten as head of the Crime Squad it was the first time he had been summoned in this way.

He had seen almost a dozen chief commissioners come and go. He had maintained more or less cordial relationships with them, and some of them had been in office such a short time that he hadn't even managed to talk to them.

Others telephoned him and asked him to their office. It nearly always had to do with some complication: getting the son or daughter of some important person out of a scrape, if it wasn't the important person himself.

His first reaction was to go to the Chief of the Police Judiciaire. He'd certainly know what was going on. At the meeting that morning, however, he hadn't said anything to Maigret, but had behaved as usual, looking vague, asking occasional questions which he didn't seem to care about.

He had been in office only three years, and, when he was nominated, the only experience with police work he could ever have had was from reading detective stories. He was a high-ranking civil servant who had been in several ministries.

Maigret remembered the time when the Chief of the Police Judiciaire was elected from among the inspectors. At one point his colleagues used to tease him by telling him he'd end up as boss.

He went out, saying anxiously to his colleagues:

"If anyone wants me, I'm with the Chief Commissioner."

At least two of the men looked up in surprise. Lucas and Janvier knew Maigret's voice better than the others and could detect the anxiety and bad humor.

His pipe in his mouth, he went down the large dusty staircase, passed under the arch, waved to the policemen on duty and walked along Quai des Orfèvres to Boulevard du Palais.

Before facing the Grand Panjandrum he almost went into the bar opposite for a drink—a beer, white wine, an apéritif, anything. Then, for the first time, he remembered that last dinner at the Pardons'—the cigarettes, the consultation near the crib.

The guards recognized him, and he stepped into the elevator.

"The Chief Commissioner's office."

"Have you got a summons?"

He showed it grudgingly. One couldn't even get in here without an appointment. He was shown to a waiting room he knew well.

"Will you wait a minute, please."

As though he had any alternative. The Chief Commissioner was new, too. Two years in office. A young man. That was the fashion. He wasn't forty yet, but after school he had accumulated enough degrees to be put at the head of any administration.

"The Sweeping Commissioner," as the newspapers nicknamed him after his first press conference. Chief commissioners, like film stars, now gave press conferences, to which they invariably invited television.

"Gentlemen, Paris must become a clean city, and to obtain this we must have it swept. In recent years too many people, too many private interests, have intervened in . . ."

Five past eleven . . . ten past eleven . . . A quarter past eleven . . . At his desk the usher with the silver chain drowsed, occasionally glancing indifferently at the Superintendent. And yet he had been in the service almost as long as Maigret.

A faint ring. The usher got up regretfully, opened the door, and beckoned, and at last the Superintendent went into a large office with velvet upholstery and Empire furniture.

"Sit down, Superintendent."

A gentle voice with an agreeable tone; a very young, thin face, fair hair. Everyone knew from the papers that on his way to the office the Chief Commissioner passed by the Roland-Garros stadium to keep himself fit with a few sets of tennis.

He gave an impression of health, vigor and also of elegance in the clothes he must have had made in London. He was smiling. In all his photographs he was smiling. His smile, admittedly, wasn't directed at anyone. He was smiling to himself with modest satisfaction

"Tell me . . ."

Just like Pardon the other night, except that instead of a cigar the Chief Commissioner was smoking a cigarette. Maybe because his wife wasn't there.

Did he have the same self-satisfied smile when his wife was there?

"I suppose you were young when you joined the police force?"

"I was twenty-two."

"How old are you now?"

"Fifty-two."

Still the same as Pardon, but probably for different reasons.

Maigret looked as sulky as possible and fiddled with his empty pipe, not daring to fill it. To tempt the devil he added:

"Three years to go before retirement."

"Exactly . . . Doesn't it seem a long time to you?"

He felt himself blushing and, to suppress his anger, he stared at the bronze legs of the desk.

"Did you start right away with the Police Judiciaire?"

The voice remained gentle and impersonal, almost an acquired gentleness.

"In my day one couldn't start with the Police Judiciaire. Like my colleagues, I started in a local police station, in the Ninth Arrondissement."

"In uniform?"

"I was the Chief Inspector's secretary. Later I worked for a time on patrol."

The Chief Commissioner was studying him with neither benevolent nor aggressive curiosity.

"Then you worked in various branches?"

12

"The métro, big stores, railway stations, morals, gambling . . ."

"You seem to have enjoyed that."

"I enjoyed school, too."

"I said that because you like talking about it."

This time Maigret went crimson.

"What do you mean?"

"Unless it's other people who talk for you. You are very well known, Monsieur Maigret, very popular."

The voice remained so gentle that it almost seemed as though the Chief Commissioner had summoned him in order to congratulate him.

"Your methods, according to the press, are fairly spectacular."

The Grand Panjandrum got up and went to the window for a minute, where he watched the cars and buses drive past the Palais de Justice. When he came toward the center of the room, his smile and his self-satisfaction had increased.

"Now that you are head of criminal investigation you still stick to your old methods. You don't spend much time in your office, I hear?"

"Not much, no, sir."

"You like to deal with matters that should normally be dealt with by your detectives. . . ."

Silence.

"Including what you term 'stakeouts.' "

This time Maigret, his teeth clenched, decided to fill his pipe.

"So you can be seen for hours on end in little bars and cafés, in thousands of places where one wouldn't expect to find an officer of your rank."

Was he going to light it? He didn't dare yet. He desisted, sitting back in his chair, while the thin, elegant Chief Commissioner walked up and down behind the mahogany desk.

"Those are archaic methods which may have been of some use in their day. . . ."

The match cracked and made the young man start, but he didn't mention it. His smile returned, the same as ever, after having disappeared for a fraction of a second.

"Members of the old police force have their own traditions. . . . Informers, for instance . . . They keep on good terms with people on the wrong side of the law; they turn a blind eye to their faults, so these people lend them a hand. . . . Do you still use informers, Monsieur Maigret?"

"Like every police force in the world."

"Do you turn a blind eye to some things?"

"When it's necessary."

"Haven't you realized that much has changed since the time you started?"

"I've been here long enough to see nine chiefs of the Police Judiciaire and eleven chief commissioners."

Too bad! It was a question of loyalty to himself and all his colleagues at the Quai—the old ones, at any rate, since the young detectives were only too ready to share the attitude of this tennis player.

If the Chief Commissioner registered the blow he didn't show it. He could have been a diplomat. Who knows? He might end up an ambassador.

"Do you know Mademoiselle Prieur?"

The real attack had started. On what ground? Maigret couldn't guess yet.

"Should I know her, sir?"

"Certainly."

"It's the first time I've heard that name."

"Mademoiselle Nicole Prieur . . . You haven't heard of Monsieur Jean-Baptiste Prieur, Head of Petitions at the State Council, either?"

"No."

"He lives at 42 Boulevard de Courcelles."

"I can't deny it."

"He's Nicole's uncle, and she lives with him."

"I take your word for it, sir."

"Now, Superintendent, tell me where you were last night at one o'clock in the morning."

This time the tone was harder and the eyes had stopped smiling.

"I'm waiting for your answer."

"Is this an interrogation?"

"That's up to you. I asked you a question."

"May I ask on what authority?"

"As your superior officer."

"All right."

Maigret took his time. He had never felt so humiliated, and his fingers clutched the bowl of his pipe until they turned white.

"I went to bed at half past ten, after watching television with my wife."

"Did you dine at home?"

"Yes."

"What time did you go out?"

"I'm coming to that, sir. A little before midnight the telephone rang."

"I suppose your number is in the directory?"

"That's right."

"Isn't it inconvenient? Doesn't that mean that every kind of person, including jokers, can get in touch with you?"

"I thought so, too. For years my number wasn't printed, but people ended up getting hold of it. After changing it five or six times I let it appear in the directory, like everyone else."

"Most useful for your informers. It also enables them to reach you personally, instead of calling the Police Judiciaire, and you get full credit for a case."

Maigret managed not to say anything.

"So you were called a little before midnight. How long before midnight?"

"I answered in the dark. The conversation went on for a long time, and when my wife turned on the light it was ten minutes to twelve."

"Who was it? Someone you knew?"

"No. A woman."

"Did she give her name?"

"Not just then."

"And not during the telephone conversation you allegedly had with her?"

"Which I *did* have with her."

"All right. Did she ask you to meet her here in town?"

"In a way, yes."

"How do you mean?"

He began to realize how stupid he had been to tell this self-satisfied greenhorn about it.

"She had just come to Paris for the first time in her life."

"What?"

"I'm telling you what she said. She added that she

was the daughter of a magistrate at La Rochelle, that she was eighteen, that she was stifling in a strict family atmosphere which was all the more intolerable since a school friend of hers, who had been in Paris for a year, had told her about the marvels of the capital."

"Original, isn't it?"

"I've had less original confessions that were just as sincere. Do you know how many girls, of allegedly good family . . ."

"I read the statistics."

"I agree there wasn't anything new about her story, and if there had been I wouldn't have bothered. She left home without telling her parents, with a suitcase of clothes and personal things, as well as her money. . . . Her friend met her at the Gare de Montparnasse. This friend wasn't alone. She was with a man of about thirty whom she introduced as her fiancé."

"The dark man the fortunetellers talk about?"

"They got into a red Lancia, and ten minutes later stopped in front of a hotel."

"Do you know which hotel it was?"

"No."

"Nor, I suppose in which arrondissement it was?"

"Exactly, sir. But I've heard more unlikely stories in the course of my career which haven't been any the less true. This girl didn't know Paris. It was her first visit. A childhood friend was waiting for her and introduced her fiancé. They drove along streets she had never seen before. They stopped in front of a shabby hotel, left her luggage, and went out to dinner. They made her drink."

Maigret recalled the pathetic voice on the telephone, the simple but credible and moving words, seemingly impossible to invent.

"I'm still slightly drunk," she admitted. "I don't even know what I've been drinking. . . . 'Come and see my apartment,' my friend told me. And they both drove me to a sort of modern studio with shocking pictures and photographs on the walls. My friend laughed. 'Scared?' she asked. 'Show her it's not so bad, Marco!' "

"Am I right in thinking she told you all this on the telephone and that you were listening in bed next to your wife?"

"Quite right, except that she gave me further details later."

"When was 'later'?"

"At some point she ran away, and realized that she was alone in Paris with neither her luggage, her hand-bag, nor her money."

"Is that when she thought of telephoning you? She obviously knew your name from the papers. She didn't have her bag but she got the money to call you from a public phone."

"From a bar she went to. She ordered a drink and asked for a coin for the telephone. Barmen don't usually make people pay in advance."

"So you flew to her aid. Why didn't you get the local police station to help her?"

Because there had been a doubt in Maigret's mind— but he didn't want to mention it. From now on he was going to say as little as possible.

"You see, Superintendent, the girl in question is not from La Rochelle and her version of the facts had nothing in common with yours. Monsieur Jean-Baptiste Prieur was worried about not seeing his niece at breakfast this morning and to hear that she wasn't in her room.

"She came back exhausted and disheveled at half past eight in the morning. What she said upset the State Councilor so much that he telephoned personally to the Minister of the Interior. When I was informed, I told a stenographer to take down Mademoiselle Prieur's statement. . . . You have three years to go before you retire, Monsieur Maigret . . ."

He remembered Pardon's words:

"Tell me, have you ever met, in the course of your career . . ."

Pure wickedness! Evil for evil's sake, perpetrated in cold blood!

But who?

"What do you expect me to do, sir? Resign?"

"I would have to accept."

"What's stopping you?"

"Read this typed statement. Let me have your version of the facts in every detail, in writing. Of course you are forbidden to importune Mademoiselle Prieur or to question anyone about her. I shall call for you when I have read your statement."

He walked to the door and held it open, still smiling slightly.

2

Maigret, scorning the elevator, was on the third or fourth step of the white marble staircase when the door opened again. It was the one-armed usher, who, unlike the Commissioner, could not play tennis every morning.

"The Chief Commissioner would like another word with you, sir."

For an instant he hesitated, not knowing whether to return or go on down. Finally he went through the anteroom again, and the Chief Commissioner himself opened his door.

"I forgot to say that I don't want any mention of this matter at the Quai des Orfèvres. Particularly since I will hold you responsible for anything that appears in the papers."

Since the Superintendent stood motionless he added a final:

"Thank you, sir."

Did he say that? Did he not say that? Maigret didn't know. He saw the usher, waved, and went down the marble staircase for the last time. In the street he was surprised to find the sun, the heat, moving men and women, the stream of cars, the colors and smells of everyday life.

He felt a spasm in his chest. He stopped and raised his hand as though he had a weak heart.

Pardon had told him not to worry about it, it was just aerophagia. But the attacks were alarming nevertheless, especially when accompanied by dizziness. Objects and passers-by became less real, like photographs out of focus.

At the corner of the street he pushed open the door of a café facing the embankment, where for years he used to drop in for a drink.

"A beer, sir?"

He was breathing with difficulty. His forehead was covered with sweat, and he looked anxiously in the mirror, past the bottles on the shelf.

"A brandy."

He was no longer flushed, but pale and staring.

"Small or large?"

"Large!" he retorted ironically.

Always because of Pardon. It was incredible how important this seemingly banal conversation he had had with his friend was becoming. The doctor had advised him to drink less, but he himself, who smoked a cigar at home to please his wife, lit a cigarette the minute he was outside.

"In all your career have you ever met . . . ?"

The vicious criminal, evil for evil's sake. He didn't even smile ironically.

21

"Another one, François . . ."

The clock said twenty to twelve. It had all happened in less than half an hour, a half hour that constituted a sort of gulf in his life. From now on there was the past and the present, before and after. After?

Images remained blurred to him. What if he collapsed here, on the floor of the café, among people drinking their apéritifs and not paying any attention to him?

Come on, Maigret! Don't be sentimental. Don't be childish. How many of the men he'd interrogated in his office felt their heart beat too fast, or thought it would stop beating? To them, too, he'd given a glass of the brandy he kept in his cabinet.

"How much is it?"

He paid. He felt hot. It really was hot. Others were also mopping their foreheads with their handkerchiefs. Why was François looking at him as though he had suddenly changed?

He wasn't even reeling. He wasn't drunk. You don't get drunk on two glasses of brandy, even double ones. He waited calmly for the green light, to cross the street and make for 38 Quai des Orfèvres.

He no longer resented that snotty Commissioner, whom, a short while ago, he would gladly have punched in the face. The Commissioner was only a pawn.

He certainly didn't like policemen of the old school. Maigret was the last of them, among the superintendents. He had seen them retire one after the other, and had had to get used to younger faces and a different attitude toward the job.

The only member of the old school who remained at the Quai des Orfèvres was Barnacle. He had been a detective when Maigret arrived, and, never having passed an exam, he always kept the same rank.

He was known as "Cold in the Head" because of his almost permanent cold, or as "The man with the big feet." He could never find shoes to fit his sensitive feet. Since he couldn't be given any of the more difficult tasks, he was the one sent peddling from door to door, like a vacuum-cleaner salesman, to interrogate the porters, or even the inhabitants of a whole street.

Poor Barnacle! Maigret had never felt so close to him. The detective was retiring in three months. And Maigret?

He raised his hand to wave to the policemen on duty, slowly went up the stairs, stopped halfway up because it seemed to him again that his heart was beating irregularly.

He went into his office, closed the door, and looked around as though the sight were unfamiliar. And yet he knew every detail. With the years, the objects had had time to set and to look eternal. He was tempted to open the cabinet with the washbasin and the bottle of brandy for his fainting clients.

Shrugging his shoulders he went through to the detectives.

"Anything new, boys?"

They looked at him as François, the bartender, had looked at him. Lucas got up.

"Another holdup at a jeweler's . . ."

"You look after that, will you?"

He hesitated, caught between reality and unreality.

"Call my wife and tell her I won't be back for lunch. And, before you leave, order me some sandwiches and beer."

His colleagues wondered what had happened to him. What could he tell them, knowing nothing himself? For the first time it was he who was being attacked and had to account for himself.

He took off his jacket, opened the other window, and sank into his chair. On his desk lay six pipes and some unopened files—doubtless papers to be signed.

He selected the biggest pipe, filled it slowly, but when it was lit, it tasted foul. He had to get up to take from his jacket pocket the document the Chief Commissioner had given him.

A stenographer had been sent to Monsieur Jean-Baptiste Prieur's house on Boulevard de Courcelles to take down his young niece's statement. The stenographer must have been a detective. From which branch?

Head of Petitions at the State Council. Maigret vaguely remembered having read the words "State Council" over a monumental door on Place du Palais-Royale. It was an important organization in the government hierarchy, but, like most Frenchmen, he only had a vague idea of its functions.

The State Council, he thought, was in charge of the constitutionality of the laws and decrees, and obviously also decided on the acceptability of complaints lodged by individuals and corporations against the state.

Head of Petitions—this meant that the person with this title had to present the complaints in question to the Council, after having studied the files, and give a warranted opinion.

"Statement of Mademoiselle Nicole Prieur, age eighteen, student, domiciled with her uncle, Monsieur Jean-Baptiste Prieur, Head of Petitions at the State Council, 42 Boulevard de Courcelles. June 28, 9:30 A.M."

Boulevard de Courcelles: large buildings opposite Parc Monceau, large doorways, chauffeurs polishing cars in the courtyards and porters in uniform like the Commissioner's usher.

"On Monday evening, after dining with my uncle, I went to see a friend, Martine Bouet, the daughter of a doctor, on Boulevard Saint-Germain. I took the métro, since my uncle was using the car. . . ."

Maigret was taking notes. After dinner, the evening before, he had watched television with Madame Maigret, without any premonition of what would happen later.

"In Martine's room we spent most of the evening listening to some new records she had been given for her birthday. Martine's mad about music. So am I, but not as much as she is. . . ."

How innocent and virginal! The two girls in the room listening to . . . Listening to what? Bach? Pop songs? Jazz?

"I left at about eleven-thirty and thought I'd go back by the métro. Once in the street, however, I wanted to walk because the night was cool and the day had been stifling. . . ."

He tried to imagine her, in the drawing room on Boulevard de Courcelles, dictating this statement, looking important. The sentences seemed out of an essay. Had her uncle been there? Had there been any corrections, any second thoughts?

"At one point I went down Rue de Seine to get to the embankment, because I love walking along the embankment, especially at night. . . . It was then that I realized I'd left two records at Martine's, which I'd brought for her to hear.

"My uncle usually goes to bed early, because he gets up at dawn. I knew he'd been out for only about an hour. I was afraid Martine would call me at home about the records. . . ."

It was possible. Everything was possible; now Maigret knew it better than ever. And yet this passage didn't sound as convincing as the beginning of the story.

"I was in front of a little café, where the proprietor was sitting by the window reading his newspaper. I remember distinctly the words painted on the window: Chez Désiré.

"An old-fashioned bistro, with a tin bar, five or six tables of varnished wood, fairly dim lighting. I went in. . . ."

Maigret was soon going to appear, and he wondered what sort of an introduction he was going to get. At that hour, the night before, he'd been sleeping innocently in the double bed next to Madame Maigret.

"I immediately asked for a token for the telephone, and the proprietor got up sullenly, as though annoyed at being disturbed. I told him to serve me coffee at any table and went into the phone booth.

"When Martine answered, we chatted for a while. She wanted to know where I was. I told her I was calling from a sweet, old-fashioned bistro where there wasn't a soul, except for the proprietor, with a large striped cat on his knees. . . . She was going to join me, but I said I wasn't staying long, that I wanted to walk the few hundred yards before catching the métro. . . ."

The detective in Maigret was coming to the surface. She must have called her friend, because the detail could be checked. She liked Chez Désiré, because that was where Maigret had joined her later. There had been, therefore, two telephone calls, one to Martine, the other to the Superintendent.

She mentioned only one token. Maigret was anxious to know if she'd mention a second one.

"We chatted together for about ten minutes, maybe a little more. We had just left each other, of course, but two girls have always got something to talk about. . . . One thinks one's finished and then one starts on another subject. . . ."

That meant that the first call hadn't been for Martine but for Maigret. It would have given him time to dress, jump into a taxi, and get to Rue de Seine.

"Then I sat at the table where my coffee had been served. The proprietor had sat down again by the window, his cat on his knees. An evening paper was lying on a chair, and, since I hadn't read it, I skimmed through it, letting my coffee cool.

"I don't know how long that took. . . ."

Here again she must have taken into account the eventual evidence of the proprietor. At that moment she must have been wondering if the Superintendent, after her act on the telephone, would come or not. The timing, at any rate, was perfect.

"Come in!" shouted Maigret.

It was the waiter from the Brasserie Dauphine, carrying a tray of sandwiches and also two bottles of beer.

"Put them there."

He wasn't hungry or thirsty. Knitting his brow he got up to close the door, which the waiter hadn't shut properly when he went out.

At any rate, one detail was true: the cup of coffee. And when he had arrived at Chez Désiré, there had indeed been an open newspaper on a chair next to the girl.

"It didn't seem very long, but I wouldn't swear to it, since my uncle's always accusing me of having no sense of time. . . . I was about to take my change purse out of my pocket. . . . I was wearing a light suit with two pockets, so I hadn't brought a bag. . . . That's another of my faults: leaving my bag everywhere. . . . So I always try to wear dresses with pockets. . . ."

Cunning. That took care of the story about the stolen handbag.

"Just then, in came a fairly tall man with broad shoulders and a heavy face. . . ."

Thanks for the compliment!

"I could be wrong, but I think he'd been looking at me for some time through the window. . . . I vaguely remember a figure pacing the pavement. . . .

"At first I thought he was coming toward me, but he sat at the next table, or, rather, sank into a chair and mopped his brow. . . . I don't know if he'd already been drinking. . . . This occurred to me. . . ."

Careful! From now on her statement would have to coincide with what the proprietor might say later.

"His face looked familiar, although I couldn't place it. . . . Then I remembered that I'd seen his photograph in the papers. . . .

"He seemed to guess what I was thinking and said to me:

" 'You're right—I am Superintendent Maigret.' "

That was a mistake. Maigret would never have said that, but the girl had to give a plausible reason for starting a conversation at once.

But Désiré, sitting on his chair, was an awkward witness.

In fact, he hadn't got up when the Superintendent came in, just glanced at him over his newspaper. One could ask why he kept his bar open. Maybe out of habit? Or to be alone and read his paper in peace instead of lying in bed with his wife?

"I'm not the sort of girl to chase after stars and celebrities to get their autographs. My uncle entertains celebrities every week on Boulevard de Courcelles.

"And yet I was pleased to see a detective at close quarters, especially the one who was most talked about. . . . I thought he'd be larger and, above all, fatter. What surprised me most was the briskness of his movements, and I immediately wondered if he'd been drinking. . . ."

There we go again! And Maigret suddenly recalled the evening at the Pardons', which was becoming ridiculously important to him. He was accused of drinking! He had been drinking now, too. Two brandies. Large ones! The waiter could testify. And there were two bottles of beer on the tray. He defiantly poured out a glass, savagely seized a sandwich, which he bit into and put down immediately.

He wasn't hungry. He was furious, plunging further into an unreal world where he was playing the main part without knowing exactly what his part was.

In a nightmare, one realizes everything is false. Even if, as long as one's asleep, one thinks one is in reality, waking up soon puts an end to the incoherence.

Here, reality was incoherent. He wasn't asleep. He wasn't dreaming. Before him he had a statement that was neither an anonymous letter nor the account of a lunatic, but an official document given to him by the Chief Commissioner of Police in person.

And the Chief Commissioner of Police believed it. Wasn't Maigret himself going to believe it, too? He recollected what had happened before this scene in the café. A telephone had rung—then the girl's voice, which he listened to in the darkness, not wanting to hang up, then Madame Maigret, who had lit the bedside lamp and asked:

"What is it?"

He shrugged, still listening to the account made in a broken, pleading voice.

Just then he was still in something secure, at home, in a room he'd lived in for more than twenty-five years. His wife was next to him, quite real, too.

She gave him a pipe he hadn't emptied before going to bed and struck a match. She knew that when he was wakened up abruptly he liked a few puffs at his pipe to revive him.

He had been in his office for a long time, too. He had thought it real, and it was already becoming less so. Who knew what would happen when Maigret gave the Commissioner his version of the facts?

What had he been told by his powerful boss, who for two years had promised to sweep Paris and played tennis every morning at Roland-Garros, where he allowed himself to be photographed?

He had, incidentally, been wickedly unjust about the Superintendent's celebrity. Maigret had never sought it. On the contrary. On how many occasions had his investigations been complicated by the fact that he was recognized everywhere? Was it his fault if the journalists had created a legend around him?

Very well! Where was he? Oh, yes . . . the Commissioner had said something like:

"So, because someone you didn't know told you a touching and unlikely story, you got up in the middle of the night to meet her in a bar. . . . As Head of the Crime Squad it didn't occur to you to send a detective to deal with the matter. . . ."

He wasn't wrong. The proof was that Madame Maigret had asked him more or less the same thing:

"Why don't you send a detective?"

Precisely because the matter wasn't clear, because the facts he was being told on the telephone were slightly incoherent. Isn't life frequently incoherent? Once again he had proof of it. Only this time he was at the center of this incoherence.

One to the Commissioner. Anyhow, Maigret wasn't angry with him any more. He no longer wanted to punch him in the face. He was just a pawn, and, at the moment, he, too, looked like an idiot.

He drained his glass, poured another, which he placed within reach, and filled his pipe before bending over the typed pages.

"He ordered some white wine. The proprietor asked:

" 'Sealed?'

"He said yes and was given a glass and a little bottle. He offered me some, too, but I told him I'd just had coffee. . . . I no longer know how he made his suggestion. Something like:

" 'Most people have a false idea of our job. I bet you do, too.'

" 'One always hears about your interrogations and the confessions you end up by extorting. . . .'

" 'That's at the end. What matters is the routine work. . . . This evening, for instance, I'm looking for a dangerous criminal I'll probably find in one of the local bars. . . .' "

Despite her pathos, the story on the telephone about her friend and the sinister Marco was more foolproof than the words she attributed to Maigret.

" 'If you'd like to come with me . . .'

"He got up, thinking I'd accept. He threw some money on the table, and, when I wanted to pay for my coffee, the proprietor said it had been paid for.

"We went out together.

" 'Are your parents expecting you?'

" 'My uncle doesn't worry about when I come in. He trusts me. . . .'

" 'Come on, then.'

"I let my curiosity get the better of me. I remember passing by Rue Jacob and going down a little street, whose name I've forgotten, into a bar where masses of people crowded around the counter.

"I looked at the faces around me, wondering if the criminal the Superintendent was looking for was one of them. He gave me a drink. It was whisky. I hesitated, but I was thirsty, since I'd just swallowed some bitter coffee, which had got cold.

"I think my glass must have been filled without my knowing it and that I drank two, thinking I was only drinking one. Everyone was standing elbow to elbow. It was hot, and the room was full of smoke.

"'Come on . . . I've only spotted a couple of pimps here. They're of no interest. . . . The man I'm after must be somewhere else.'

"'I'd rather go home.'

"'Give me another half hour and you'll be able to watch a sensational arrest. It'll be in the headlines tomorrow. . . .'"

For the story to ring true, he'd have to have time to make her drunk. She had to be fairly vague, so that it would be impossible to find the places where she'd been taken. The two stories, finally, had to be superimposable, one as false as the other, but with the same points of contact with reality.

"The second place was in a basement, and jazz was being played. People were dancing. . . . I don't know the night clubs of Saint-Germain-des-Près, but I suppose this was one of them. . . . The Superintendent gave me another drink. . . . I wasn't myself. I reeled, and I thought a drink would do me good. . . .

"Then everything became more and more blurred, and there are large blanks in my memory. . . . On the sidewalk he held me around the waist, pretending I might fall. . . . I tried to push him away. . . . He made me go through a door, along a badly lighted hall. He spoke to someone at a desk, an unshaven old man with white hair.

"I remember narrow stairs, red velvet upholstery, rooms with numbers, the Superintendent turning a key. . . .

"I repeated automatically:

"'No! . . . No! . . . I don't want to. . . .'

He laughed. We were in a room, near a bed.

" 'Leave me! . . . Leave me, or I'll call . . .'

"I could swear he replied:

" 'You're forgetting that I'm the police!' "

It was almost true. Not the last sentence, of course. And the girl hadn't struggled. Maigret hadn't taken her from one bar to another, either, and hadn't given her anything to drink.

What was true was the meeting at Chez Désiré and some of the things they'd said. At that moment the girl's Christian name had indeed been Nicole, but she pretended her surname was Carvet and that she was the daughter of a magistrate at La Rochelle. Her friend, who had met her at the station with Marco, was named Laure Dubuisson, the daughter of a fish seller in the same town.

"If I'm not mistaken, you neither know where your friend lives, nor where you were driven, nor where you left your luggage. And you'd be incapable of recognizing the building from which you fled leaving your handbag with all your money. . . ."

She was still drunk and her breath smelled of liquor.

"The main thing is to find you a bed for the night. . . . Come on . . ."

It was true that he'd thrown money on the table. True, too, that on Boulevard Saint-Germain he'd held her arm, and, slightly later, when she started reeling still more, he'd held her by the waist.

He knew a decent, cheap hotel, the Hotel de Savoie, on Rue des Ecoles. They hadn't stopped on the way, despite Nicole's accusations.

"How could you write to your friend if you didn't know her address?"

In a dull voice, she replied:

"You think I'm lying, telling stories, don't you? I wrote to her *Poste Restante!* Laure always loved mystery. At school she used to pretend . . ."

He didn't remember what Laure used to pretend. He was hardly listening, eager to get rid of her.

It was true that the unshaven night porter of the Hotel de Savoie had white hair, and that he'd handed over a key, mumbling:

"The second floor, on the left."

There was no elevator.

"Help me climb the stairs . . . I can hardly stand."

He had helped her, and now he could make out only where truth ended and fantasy began.

"I can't manage it, Monsieur Maigret. . . . I'm very drunk, aren't I? I'm so ashamed. I'll never dare go back to my parents."

They got to the second floor, and Maigret did turn the key in the lock.

"Go to sleep and don't worry. I'll see to things in the morning."

In the room she tripped, fell to the floor, and made no attempt to get up. In a few minutes she'd be asleep.

He lifted her up, took off her shoes and her jacket. He was going to leave her when she groaned:

"I'm thirsty."

He went into a tiny bathroom, rinsed out a mug, and filled it with cold water. When he came back, she was sitting on the bed, trying to take off her skirt.

"My belt's hurting. . . ."

She drank, looking at him in distress.

"Won't you help me? . . . If you knew how ill I am! . . . I think I'm going to be sick. . . ."

He helped her undress, but she remained in her underclothes.

She wasn't sick.

"Well?" Madame Maigret had asked him when he got home.

"An odd story . . . We'll see tomorrow. . . ."

"Is she pretty?"

"I must admit I didn't notice. . . . She was plastered."

"What did you do with her?"

"I took her to a hotel, where I had to put her to bed."

"Did you undress her?"

"I had to."

"Aren't you scared?"

Madame Maigret had antennae. He wasn't happy either.

At nine o'clock, on arriving at his office, he called the Hotel de Savoie, where he was told that the occupant of room 32 had left, saying that Superintendent Maigret, who had brought her, would pay her bill.

Ten minutes later the policeman on telephone duty told him there was no magistrate named Carvet in La Rochelle and that there was no Carvet in the telephone directory. No Dubuisson either.

3

"You're forgetting that I'm the police!"

Maigret was standing by the open window, his hands thrust in his pockets, his teeth clamped on the stem of his pipe. He hadn't the courage to reread Nicole Prieur's statement. For a long time he had remained sunk in his chair, exhausted, disheartened, without any fight left. For a long time he had felt like a stranger in his office, vaguely noticing the noise of voices and the people coming and going in the detectives' room.

He had three years to go before retirement. Pardon, too, had emphasized it. Why? Because he looked tired? Because Pardon had found there was something wrong with him and didn't want to tell him about it?

He had told him to drink less, or, rather, not to drink at all. A little wine at meals. Soon he would be put on a diet. Then given pills to take at various times. He was on the threshold of old age, when one after the other the organs became fragile or defaulted, like old cars whose parts have to be changed continuously. Except that men can't buy spare parts yet.

He was unaware of the passage of time. The spots of sunlight in the office, on the upholstery and the wall, changed places without his noticing them.

He had neither fight left nor any wish to defend himself. He accepted defeat. For some time he even felt a certain relief. No more responsibility. No more exhausting nights hammering away at a man whose confession would put the finishing touch to an investigation.

"You're forgetting that I'm the police!"

Maybe that's what saved him. He was nearly at Meung-sur-Loire, where the house was ready for them, his wife and him, with a garden he would cultivate just as his neighbors did, with flowers and the vegetables he would water peacefully at sunrise and sunset, with his fishing rods in the shed . . .

"You're forgetting that I'm the police!"

It was so out of character, it sounded so false, that a smile spread across his face, and in a moment he slowly drew himself up. On his feet, he looked at the sandwiches he had disdained. He took one, chewed a mouthful, and opened the last bottle of beer. He ate, standing by the window, watching the Seine through the motionless leaves of the trees on the bank.

He was at last in touch with the outside world, with the passers-by on their way somewhere, a young couple hugging each other, who were slowly crossing the Pont Saint-Michel, stopping in the middle to watch a string of barges, to see the water flowing, to look at anything, because all that mattered was the happiness they expressed by hugging each other.

Typewriters rattled next door. From time to time the detectives must have looked questioningly at the chief's office and exchanged worried glances.

He went back to his desk to read the last sentence of Nicole Prieur's statement, because there still was one more sentence.

"He didn't take advantage of me. I suppose at the last moment he lost his nerve. . . ."

He filled his pipe, went back to the window, with more determination, a light in his eyes. Then, after heaving a sigh, he went at last to open the door of the next office.

Lucas was away. Many of the others, too, were scattered around Paris. Young Lapointe was on vacation. Janvier was typing a report. They all knew he was there, looking at them, but, out of discretion, they didn't dare raise their heads, because they knew that if the Superintendent shut himself up like that something serious must be going on.

The clock said three.

"Will you come in with your pad, Janvier?"

Besides Lapointe, Janvier was the best stenographer in the squad, and he came into the office at once, shutting the door behind him. His expression betrayed a question he dared not ask.

"Sit down . . . I'll dictate."

It didn't take as long as he would have thought. An hour earlier he would have provided explanations, formulated theories. Now he stuck to the facts, avoiding anything resembling a commentary.

As his account continued, Janvier became more serious, knitted his brows, occasionally glancing anxiously at his chief.

Twenty minutes were enough.

"Type out three copies."

"Yes, chief."

Maigret hesitated for a few seconds. The Commissioner had called him back to his office to warn him not to talk about it to anybody.

"Read this."

He pushed over the girl's statement. After twenty lines Janvier blushed as Maigret had blushed that morning at Police Headquarters.

"Who on earth could . . . ?"

Good old Janvier! He and Lucas were Maigret's oldest colleagues, and the three men no longer needed words to understand each other.

Immediately, without having to think, Janvier asked the same question that Maigret had taken longer to ask, because he was directly implicated.

"Who?"

"That's what I'd like to know. . . . Who?"

They were used to young ladies who were more or less nymphomaniacs, more or less hysterical, who came periodically to try out their little games at the Quai des Orfèvres. There were some regular attendants, too, who reappeared on certain days, like the so-called moonlight murderers, dear to the newspapers.

Maigret had, of course, envisaged this possibility, but a lunatic would never have played this double game without making a single mistake. Whoever played this double game must have been taught it.

"While you're typing this report, I'm going to make an experiment, and I think I know the result."

Janvier had guessed it, too.

"Don't mention this matter to your colleagues. The

Grand Panjandrum thinks it's a state secret. If you've got time, try to find out about Monsieur Jean-Baptiste Prieur."

Just as Maigret was about to leave the room, Janvier murmured:

"I hope you're not going to worry, chief."

"I offered to resign."

"Did he accept?"

"He said he should accept, but that . . ."

"Well?"

"I'm staying. As long as I'm not fired. I've decided to defend myself."

He took a taxi first to Rue de Seine, where he nonchalantly opened the door of Chez Désiré. The owner was behind the bar, serving a group of plasterers in white overalls who were drinking red wine. In a corner a middle-aged man was writing a letter, a cup of coffee in front of him.

Désiré recognized his client of the evening before at a glance, but he didn't show it, avoided looking him in the face, and busily fiddled about with glasses and bottles.

"A small glass of white wine . . . Not sealed, this time."

The man, with bulging eyes and a mauve complexion, apparently exhausted by the heat, put a glass on the bar and juggled with a bottle.

"Sixty centimes."

The plasterers took no notice of Maigret. Nor did the man writing his letter, who was having trouble with his ball-point pen.

"Say . . ."

Désiré turned toward him reluctantly.

"Did I leave anything behind last night? Did I leave my umbrella?"

"Nobody left an umbrella."

"Do you remember the girl who waited for me after she'd phoned me? Did she ask you for one or two tokens?"

The owner remained stubbornly silent for a few moments.

"That's none of my business. Anyhow, I can't remember what happened last night, and I don't have to talk about it."

"Did someone come around this morning and tell you not to talk?"

The workmen were now listening, looking at the Superintendent, examining him from head to foot.

"That's sixty centimes," the old fool repeated.

Maigret put one franc on the bar and went toward the door.

"You've forgotten your change. . . . I don't accept tips. . . ."

That was just about what happened at the Hotel de Savoie on Rue des Ecoles. The manageress was a plump woman with hair dyed red, who retained a certain charm. She was in the office, near a board of keys.

"Good morning."

He could tell at a glance that she knew who he was. He introduced himself just the same.

"Superintendent Maigret, from the Police Judiciaire."

"Yes?"

"Last night I brought a girl here, and I've come to pay for the room, because she hadn't any money."

"You don't owe me anything."

"Did she pay?"

"That doesn't matter. You don't owe me anything."

"So someone came this morning to pay for her room and interrogate the night porter?"

"Look, Superintendent, I know who you are and I haven't got anything against you, but I don't want any trouble. I know nothing about this person and I don't know what you're talking about. My accounts are in order. The police have never had any trouble with us, nor has the tax inspector."

"Thank you."

"I'm sorry I can't be of more help."

"I quite understand."

Precautions had been taken. There was no point in telephoning Martine Bouet, the friend with whom Mademoiselle Prieur had spent the evening listening to records. She wouldn't answer either. He was almost sure, moreover, that, from Chez Désiré, Nicole had telephoned to Boulevard Saint-Germain.

The Commissioner wasn't the one who had rigged this one. He didn't appreciate policemen of the old school, and it was his right. He especially disliked Maigret because the papers spoke too much of him. That was his right, too.

The Minister of the Interior had called him that morning in a panic to tell him about a matter that might be awkward for both of them.

Those people were neither heroes nor saints. They had got to their posts only through a succession of intrigues they preferred to forget about and they had to pocket a few affronts to stay where they were.

Maigret was implicated in a shady matter, if not in a

scandal. An influential dignitary of the state had lodged a complaint and threatened to approach higher circles.

It was quite human. And how satisfactory for the Sweeping Commissioner to haul up an older man, more popular than himself, and tell him, in a soft voice, a few home truths!

Paris was sizzling in the sun. Many of the shutters were closed against the heat. Here and there men were fishing, and there were other lovers besides those on the Pont Saint-Michel, two, in particular, who had removed their shoes and dangled their bare feet over the water. They laughed, watching their toes move grotesquely.

"Janvier!"

"Coming, chief."

He was on the telephone. When he went into Maigret's office, he held some typed pages. The Superintendent started reading them. He read only four or five lines.

"Are you sure you haven't left anything out?"

"I checked it. But I'd rather . . ."

"No!" Maigret had no wish to be confronted with his own words. He signed with a heavy pen, took an official envelope, addressed it, and rang for the usher.

"To be delivered by hand to the Commissioner's office . . .

"Go on, Janvier . . ."

"I called a friend of mine who's a lawyer and fairly highly thought of in administrative circles."

"Does he know Prieur?"

"He's a brilliant jurist, apparently one of the best of

44

our time. He was married, and his wife was killed in a car accident about ten years ago. His father was a shipowner . . ."

"At La Rochelle?"

"You've guessed it."

They both smiled. It's rare for somebody who's lying to invent the whole time. The girl who told him such a poignant story on the telephone said she was from La Rochelle. His father was a magistrate and her friend the daughter of a fish seller.

"Go on."

"He's still got a brother down there who takes care of the ships. As for him, he's got a personal fortune and has a large apartment on Boulevard de Courcelles. Another brother, Christophe, who was married, had a daughter, and lived in Morocco, committed suicide in circumstances my friend knows nothing about. His wife disappeared. She's thought to have married an American and to be living in Texas. As for the daughter, it's the Nicole Prieur you know."

"Anything else?"

"The young lady, who passed her school-leaving exams last year, goes to lectures at the Sorbonne."

"What sort of girl?"

"My friend hasn't met her, but he thinks his wife has seen her. He'll ask her when he gets home."

There was no reason for Monsieur Jean-Baptiste Prieur, Head of Petitions at the State Council and an eminent jurist, to bear a grudge against a Maigret whom he'd probably never even heard of, and still less to set a trap for him in which his niece's honor was at stake.

"I'd give a lot to have a talk with the girl."

"I'm afraid they won't let you, chief."

"Can't you think of anyone interested enough in getting rid of me to think all this up?"

"You're obviously getting in a number of people's way. . . . Just to mention the ones who for two months have been robbing jewelers in broad daylight . . . Again this morning, on Avenue Victor-Hugo . . ."

"Did they leave any traces?"

"None."

"Did they shoot?"

"No. They left quietly by car, and no one reacted, not even the jeweler, who was so staggered, standing behind the counter, that it took him a minute to press the alarm bell. . . . Are you thinking about something?"

"Maybe . . . Where was I yesterday at eleven o'clock?"

Janvier knew because he had driven the little black car.

"At Manuel's."

"And . . ."

Three times in a week Maigret had been to see Manuel Palmari, the old owner of the Clou Doré on Rue Fontaine, who now lived like a well-off retiree in his bourgeois apartment on Rue des Acacias.

"It might be stupid, but I'd like to ask him a few more questions."

It seemed insane, but hadn't last night's events been just as insane?

Palmari, commonly known as Manuel by people in his group, had reigned for thirty years in Montmartre, where he had started as a young pimp.

Had he gone in for any other activities since that period when Maigret, who was young then, too, had known him? The Superintendent, who was then a detective, had suspected it without being able to pin anything on him.

During these thirty years, plenty of vagrants had disappeared from the Pigalle district. Some had been killed by rivals; others, after a few years in prison, had been sent away; others kept slightly shady restaurants somewhere between Marseilles and Nice.

Manuel, who had soon done pretty well for himself, had found a way of buying the Clou Doré, which was a shabby bar at the time, rather like Désiré's, except that it was full of crooks.

It was turned into a modern bar, then into a restaurant, with a few tables. The clients, who were no longer so young, arrived in large American cars.

Maigret sometimes used to eat there, and waited for the last client to leave the little room, which was decorated in red and gold.

"Say, Manuel . . ."

"Yes, Superintendent."

"The fellow with a scar near his eye, who was sitting in the corner . . ."

"You know, I just see the clients come in and out, I give them their grub and drink, I take their dough, and that's that."

Manuel was a born actor. He acted as much for his own benefit as for that of others, and sometimes, pleased with his performance, he'd wink at his listener.

"We've known each other for some time, haven't we?"

"We were thinner then, weren't we, Monsieur Maigret?"

"And you didn't have a sou."

"I did have a rough time of it—that's quite true—and that's why I've always kept out of trouble."

"Either that or because you were too cunning."

"You think I'm cunning, do you? I hardly went to school and I can only just read the papers."

"Manuel!"

"Yes?"

"The fellow with the scar . . ."

"All right! . . . I see what you're driving at. . . . I haven't got anything to say about it. He didn't have that scar two months ago. Two months ago—that was March . . . and in March . . ."

In March there had been a fight between two gangs in the Pigalle district, and there had been some shooting; a dead man was left on the pavement, and two wounded men had mysteriously escaped.

The Sweeping Commissioner, who played tennis and swore to clean Paris, didn't like informers and the old methods revolted him.

It was precisely to see an informer that Maigret was being driven by Janvier—to see Manuel, who, three years ago, as he was opening the door of the Clou Doré, in the small hours of the morning, to lower the blind, had received half a dozen machine-gun bullets in his thigh and stomach.

He soon managed to get transferred from the hospital he had been taken to, to one of the best private clinics in Neuilly. Everybody, starting with the doctors, was convinced he wouldn't get out alive.

At Neuilly, too, Maigret had gone to see him several times.

"I feel sorry for you, Superintendent. . . . You see, the only thing wrong with you policemen is that you never believe anyone. . . . There must have been two men in the car—that's for sure—because you can't fire a machine-gun and hold the steering wheel at the same time. . . . But, I give you my word of honor, I didn't see them for the simple reason that I had my back to them. . . .

"When you're lowering a blind, you have your back to the street, don't you?"

"You hadn't lowered it yet. You'd only just opened the door."

"But I was facing in. . . . You've been to school. Work it out . . . Some guys try to kill me. Thanks to them I'm told I'll never be able to walk again. I'll spend the rest of my life in a wheelchair like an old dotard. . . . All right! Do you think I don't want to see those guys in jail?"

He didn't talk. Maigret expected this. A few weeks later two young vagrants were killed near Toulon, vagrants who had left Paris in a hurry, shortly after the gunfight.

"You know, Superintendent, those guys come and go as they please. If you had to count all the ones who suddenly discover the air in Paris isn't doing them any good . . ."

The car drove up the Champs-Elysées, around the Arc de Triomphe, down Avenue MacMahon, to turn left into Rue des Acacias.

The district was bourgeois and peaceful; an occasional small private house with a mellowed façade stood between two apartment houses.

"Shall I come up with you, chief?"

"No . . . Look for your colleague. . . . I don't know who's on duty today."

"Lourtie, the fat man."

"You'll find him somewhere around. . . . He'll be able to tell you what Aline's been doing this morning."

Aline was a character, too. At the time of the Clou Doré, she served in the restaurant, a thin girl, her black hair on end, flashing dark eyes. She was known to be the mistress of Manuel, who had picked her up in the street.

At the clinic he had got her a small adjoining room. It was she who, on his instructions, had found a manager for the Clou Doré and occasionally went to look the restaurant over and check the accounts.

In three years she had lost her angular look and put on weight. Her mop of hair was no longer on end and, dressed with subdued elegance, she looked like a "little lady."

The building was unobtrusive, comfortable, with a large silent elevator with mahogany doors. Maigret pressed the fourth-floor button, then rang at the door on the left. He waited a fairly long time for the light sound of the rubber-tired wheelchair coming from the far end of the apartment.

"Who's there?" asked Manuel, through the door.

"Maigret."

"Again!"

The door opened.

"Come in . . . I'm alone. . . . I was having a snooze when you rang."

Manuel's hair was now a silky white, giving his face

a certain dignity. He wore an immaculate white shirt, silk trousers and red slippers.

"Well, for a man who's known me so long and for whom I've done so many favors .. No! . . . Don't let's stay in the sitting room. . . . I wonder why I've got a sitting room, because it's not my style and I never see anyone."

He had a place to himself, a little room looking out onto the street. There was a television set, a record player, two or three radios of various sizes, newspapers, magazines and hundreds of thrillers. A red couch stood in a corner next to an armchair covered in the same satin.

Manuel didn't smoke. He had never smoked. He didn't drink either.

"You know I don't like wasting my breath, but I warn you that one of these days I'm going to get cross. I'm a free citizen, with no police record. My restaurant on Rue Fontaine's duly licensed, and I pay my taxes to the last sou. . . . I live here like a mouse in a hole. . . . Because of my leg I can't leave the apartment, and I have to be undressed and washed like a baby, put to bed and taken out of it . . ."

Maigret knew his man, and waited for the end of the act. At the moment, Manuel was playing it close.

"My telephone, there, next to you, is tapped. . . . Don't deny it. I wasn't born yesterday. . . . Nor were you . . . I couldn't care less about my conversations being recorded. But that Aline should be bothered is another matter."

"Has someone bothered her?"

"Come, come, Monsieur Maigret . . . You're cleverer than I. . . ."

"I have my doubts about that."

"Well? You think that I, who can hardly read or write . . ." His favorite theme. He was as proud of it as others are of their degrees!

Maigret pulled on his pipe, smiling, and murmured:

"If I were as clever as you, Manuel, you know you'd have been in jail for ages."

"There! The same old thing . . . But to go back to Aline . . . Today a big fat man's trailing her. Yesterday, a small dark man. Tomorrow another one. She can't buy two cutlets and some cheese without one of your men on her heels.

"You're all right, granted, and I'm fond of you, which is no reason for you to come and see me nearly every day, as though I were a sick relative. . . . Why not bring me some candy and flowers? . . . If only you could tell me once and for all what you want to know . . ."

"Today it's a personal matter."

"Personal for whom?"

"Do you know Nicole?"

"Nicole who? Every street in Paris is full of Nicoles. . . . What does your one do?"

"She goes to the Sorbonne."

"What?"

"To the university, if you'd rather."

"And I'm supposed to know a girl who goes to the university?"

"I'm asking you a question. . . . She's called Nicole Prieur."

"Never heard of her."

"She lives with her uncle, near here, on Boulevard de Courcelles. . . . This uncle, Jean-Baptiste Prieur, is Head of Petitions at the State Council."

Manuel's amazement was genuine, or else he was an even better actor than Nicole herself.

"Are you serious? . . . But, for God's sake, I don't even know what the State Council is! . . . Do you think I know the top brass . . . ?"

"You don't even know Désiré, who owns a bar on Rue de Seine?"

"That's the first I've heard of him."

"Or the two kids who were operating this morning on Avenue Victor Hugo?"

Manuel sat up in his wheelchair.

"Just a minute now! If that's what you're getting at, and if you've told me that rot to catch me out . . . I've given you a clue from time to time. All right! . . . You can't own a bar in Pigalle without being in with the police. . . .

"I listen to the radio like everyone else . . . so I know what happened in the place you mentioned. . . . What would I have to do with it? For three years I haven't moved, and nobody, or practically nobody, has ever come to see me. . . . I'd be interested to know how, under those circumstances, I could still be leading a gang. . . .

"Last time you came to see me, about another jeweler, on Boulevard Saint-Martin . . . and the time before . . ."

"Where's Aline?"

"She's gone shopping."

"In the neighborhood?"

"I don't know. . . . If you really want to know, she's gone to buy some underpants and brassières. . . . Your detectives will be able to confirm it tonight."

"Did she go out this morning?"

"This morning she went to see the dentist, opposite. . . . If his window had been open, I could have seen her from my wheelchair."

Opposite, instead of an apartment house was a private house, with one floor under some attics. The house was built of stone that had turned a dark gray. The slate of the roof had the same blue-and-pink sheen in the sun as the Seine at certain times of day.

"Has she had something wrong with her teeth for long?"

"For three days . . ."

If Aline had been to the dentist before, Maigret would have known from the report of the detectives who had been trailing her for three weeks.

"What's his name?"

"Who?"

"The dentist."

"You can see his nameplate from here. . . . I can't read that far away. . . . She told me there was a dentist opposite, and I didn't find out his name. . . . All I know is that his assistant, or his nurse, if you prefer, is a big gawk of a woman I wouldn't go to bed with for anything on earth. . . . Ah! Here's Aline."

He was sharp of hearing. Despite the sitting room and the hall between them and the front door, Manuel had heard the key in the lock.

4

The door of the sitting room was open, and they saw
Aline coming across with firm, swift steps, perched on
her stiletto heels, wearing a suit of orange linen, her
black hair neatly set. In one hand she held a bag as
black as her hair, and in the other some packages, one
of which bore the name of a lingerie shop on the Lido,
and another the name of a shop on Rue Marbeuf.

She had seen Maigret in the distance, but didn't
blink, made no sign of recognizing him, and, when she
came into the room where the two men were sitting,
she passed him as though he didn't exist, bent down
and kissed Manuel on the forehead.

"Well, Daddy, so he's still here?"

She was twenty-two. Palmari was nearly sixty. And
yet the "Daddy" was by no means filial. On Aline's lips
it was an affectionate nickname, and the smile of the
former proprietor of the Clou Doré seemed to say:

"You see what sort of a woman she is?"

The fact is that the girl who had started on the sidewalks of Boulevard Sébastopol at the age of sixteen was now taken for an elegant housewife, for the young wife of some doctor, engineer or lawyer.

"He'll soon be bringing his pajamas and slippers, not to mention his toothbrush and razor. . . ."

She spoke without looking at the Superintendent, in a high-pitched voice with a strong suburban accent. She exaggerated it at will, just as Manuel played his parts. They were like two actors exchanging cues, knowing their parts backward.

What an odd girl! Dark though she was, with her chestnut-colored eyes and sunburned skin, she wasn't from the South but from a little village in Morbihan, from which she had come to Paris as a nursemaid.

She had worked for about six months with a very rich family in Neuilly who hadn't hesitated to entrust her with a little girl of three and a baby in the cradle even after she had started frequenting the dance halls in the Gravilliers district and on Rue de Lappe.

She had thrown her packages on the sofa and went on, still emphasizing her suburban accent:

"What does he want now?"

"Don't be nasty to him, Aline. You know the Superintendent's a friend of mine."

"A friend of yours, maybe. But he bores me stiff, and I hate the smell of his filthy pipe."

Maigret didn't take offense but puffed slowly at his pipe as he watched her. He suspected that it was she who, remembering her former employers, had wanted this comfortable bourgeois flat, while Manuel would have been quite happy with the dark mezzanine apartment he used to live in above his restaurant.

She must have longed for respectability.

"Do you know anyone who works at the State Council?" the invalid asked, with a note of irony.

"If it's him who's asking you, tell him I don't even know what it is. . . . You'll notice that he's squinting at my packages. I bet he'll soon be asking me what's in them. . . . Maybe he's just a pervert who gets a kick out of fiddling with women's underclothes."

The telephone rang. The man in the little wheelchair frowned, looked at the telephone, and then at the Superintendent.

"Hello . . . What? . . . Yes, he's here. . . . It's for you, Monsieur Maigret."

"What did I say? Next thing we know he'll be having his mail sent to us."

"Hello . . . Yes . . . I'm listening."

It was Janvier, who was calling from a little café on the street.

"I'm calling you as a precaution, chief. Lourtie's next to me. . . . The girl shook him off. . . . When she left her house she walked straight to the Ternes métro station. She got a first-class ticket and went down to the platform of the line going to the Etoile. Lourtie followed her. When she got into the car, he slipped in through the other door. Just as the doors shut she jumped onto the platform, and Lourtie couldn't get out in time. . . . He's come back here and she's just got in by taxi. . . ."

"Thanks."

"Is everything going as you hoped?"

"No."

She was sitting on the sofa near the two packages and, her legs crossed, still looking at Manuel and not at the guest to whom she seemed to have sworn not to speak, she said:

"It's the cop on duty. . . . They work in shifts, but I'm beginning to recognize them. Today it's a fat, puffy one, just about to have a stroke."

"Tell me, my dear . . ."

"Why's he being so familiar, Daddy? Did you say he could talk to me like that?"

"Shall I call you 'mademoiselle'?"

"Wouldn't it be better if he called me 'madame'?"

He was being teased, and Manuel, proud of the girl he had formed, looked at her tenderly.

"I promise you, Aline, he doesn't mean us any harm."

"Why did you shake off the detective who was following you?"

"I suppose he's never changed his mind at the last minute?"

She was still talking to Manuel.

"At first I was going to the Galeries Lafayette. Then, once in the métro I thought I could get what I wanted just as well in the neighborhood. . . . He can take a look. . . . He can even touch them. . . . I'll get off with washing my panties and brassières before wearing them. . . ."

The little battle had started long before her time. It had started between Palmari and the Superintendent when the young scoundrel, still skinny and penniless, had paid for the bar on Rue Fontaine in cash. As though by chance, this happened a few weeks after a holdup in a jeweler's.

For the first time, the criminals had adopted a technique that was to prove lucrative, but seemed incredibly daring. Two men broke the shop window with a hammer, seized the jewels in handfuls, taking no notice of the passers-by, who were too astonished to react, or of the jeweler, who simply gesticulated in the shop. They then jumped into a car where an accomplice waited for them, and plunged into the traffic.

Neither the jewels nor the perpetrators of the crime were ever found. Within two years about ten operations of the same kind took place, until the police caught one of the robbers, an inexperienced boy named Genaro, who didn't squeal and got five years.

Palmari, increasingly prosperous, turned his bar into an elegant café and then into an expensive restaurant.

"Business is good" was all he said to Maigret as the latter was about to question him with an innocent look. "And I'm not doing too badly on the horses. . . ."

And it was true that on Sundays he closed his establishment to go to Auteuil, Longchamp or Vincennes, according to the season.

Three times the perpetrators of robberies of jewelers had been arrested. They were nearly all clients of the Clou Doré. None of them had talked or said how they were going to dispose of the merchandise.

For two, three, four years nothing happened. Then jewel robberies began again in the same style, with men whose descriptions differed from their predecessors', as though a new gang had been formed by their leader.

"Look, my dear . . ."

"I'm his dear again! Ask him if we've slept together."

"That'll do! . . . I can come back with a warrant, or, if you'd rather, take you off and question you in my office. . . . Do you know a certain Nicole Prieur?"

She thought it over and turned once more to Manuel.

"Do you know her? The name doesn't mean anything to me."

"A girl who lives on Boulevard de Courcelles with her uncle, some big shot."

"Do you know any big shots, apart from the Superintendent, Daddy?"

"Very well! . . . I'll be back. . . . I'll just tell you both something, and Manuel at least will understand. Somewhere in Paris there are some people who have decided to get rid of me—or perhaps one person. . . ."

Aline was just about to make another joke, but her lover looked at her severely. He was suddenly interested.

"Do they want to do you in?"

"No. They want me to resign, or, rather, to retire. . . ."

"That would help a lot of people."

Aline couldn't resist adding in her high-pitched voice:

"You're telling me! I'd be the first of them!"

"Go on, Superintendent."

"They put a girl on me."

"Did it work?"

"No."

"I'd be surprised if it had. I remember having tried it on you once."

"The result's the same. They put on a clever enough performance for it to look as though I had chased after her in a disgusting way."

"Nicole What's-her-name?"

"Yes."

Maigret, becoming more serious, looked Manuel in the eye.

"I must be getting in somebody's way, somebody I'm about to catch red-handed or who thinks I am. . . ."

He paused, and Manuel, also becoming serious, repeated:

"Go on."

"It must be somebody very intelligent, who knows my habits and the methods of the police. . . . Somebody who thinks he's being followed and who tells himself that if he can get rid of me he'll be all right. . . . Does that remind you of anyone, Manuel?"

Aline didn't say a word, feeling that she shouldn't interrupt the two men. What they were talking about was beyond her.

"It could be a pervert . . ." Manuel began.

"I thought that. I also thought about revenge. I've been through the list of cases I've dealt with recently, and even the ones I've had in the last few years. None of the people in question would have both the motive and the means of hatching the plot."

"Are you asking my advice?"

"You know perfectly well that the police have been after you for some time."

"And that you have Aline followed in the street . . . I still wonder why. . . ."

"Perhaps you'll find out one day."

"If you don't resign, that is?"

"Exactly."

"So that you suspect me of having hatched the plot with this girl, some big shot's niece. . . ."

"I came to see you just in case."

There was an impressive silence.

"Do you know anyone capable of hatching this kind of plot, Manuel?"

"I know some people who would like to have a shot at you, but it would never occur to them to involve you in a scandal. . . ."

He added, after clearing his throat:

"As for me, maybe I'm no saint, but I swear on Aline's head that I didn't know anything about this business before you arrived. . . . As for the rest of it, we'll see about that."

It came as a surprise to hear the young woman's voice again. She didn't address Manuel any more. The tone was no longer high-pitched and irritating. The accent had almost vanished.

"Maybe if you told me what happened it would give me some idea. . . . When you're dealing with a woman, it's often best to ask another woman."

The Sweeping Commissioner would probably have choked with indignation if he knew that a Superintendent, Head of the Crime Squad, was confiding in a former prostitute and in a man who, rightly or wrongly, was considered one of the gang leaders of the underworld.

Maigret told them briefly about his adventure. Aline didn't smile. As the story continued she knitted her brow more and more, and sat motionless on the edge of the sofa, her legs crossed, her chin in her hands.

"Have you got a photograph of her?"

"No."

"And you haven't yet been to Boulevard de Courcelles to question her alone?"

"I'm not allowed to."

"Well, she must be cornered!"

Maigret suddenly turned toward her, struck by her remark.

"Why cornered?"

"Put yourself in her shoes . . . There's a girl of good family, rich, living with an uncle who's an influential gentleman, and so on and so forth. . . . She's never seen you. She obviously knows you only from reading your name in the papers. . . .

"Nevertheless, she plays a part that could go wrong. . . . She gets home at eight in the morning, knowing her uncle is waiting for her around the corner in a rage and is going to bombard her with questions. . . . How old did you say the girl was?"

"Eighteen."

"That's the right age. If you want my opinion, that girl's mad about a man who can wind her around his little finger. . . . He told her what to say and set the scene. . . . When you get hold of him . . ."

She added with a touch of admiration:

"When those young ladies get started, they're worse bitches than whores. . . . What do you think, Daddy?"

"I agree. . . . I don't like it."

Did they look at each other and laugh when Maigret was going down the stairs? The Superintendent could have sworn they didn't. He had left them quite worried.

As for him, he hadn't found anything out and didn't feel pleased with himself as he searched for the bar where the two detectives waited for him. He found it at once, next to the dentist's house.

"A beer!"

He was thirsty. So much the worse for Pardon. He began to resent the doctor for their conversation the week before. The doctor had told him to take care, implying that he was gradually becoming an old man who would soon be able only to fish in the Loire. The Commissioner would have been delighted.

"I'm sorry, chief," muttered Lourtie, leaning against the bar. "I couldn't tell the woman was going to . . ."

"That's all right."

"Shall I stay?"

"Wait to be relieved . . . Come on, Janvier."

And, a little later, when they were in the car:

"Drive down Boulevard de Courcelles."

He looked at the numbers. Number 24 was just opposite the main gate of Parc Monceau, the railings of which were ornamented with golden arrowheads. One could hear the shouts of children supervised by a guard in a blue uniform. The building was enormous. On either side of the vast entrance stood two men, and it was possible to imagine the teams of horses that used to prance into the courtyard, where the stables had now been turned into garages.

A fortress. That was what Maigret called these houses, in his heart of hearts. Instead of a concierge, there was a man in livery, and he certainly couldn't catch the smell of a stew cooking. The staircase must have been marble, the apartments huge, with high ceilings, and covered with carpets to muffle the sound of steps.

These blocks of apartments in smart areas had deeply impressed him when he first arrived in Paris. The butlers still wore striped jackets, the maids lace bonnets, the nurses, who pushed baby carriages in the park, English uniforms.

Since then he had frequently been obliged to carry out investigations in these houses and he had always retained the same feeling of embarrassment, maybe almost of aggressiveness, which did not stem from envy anyway.

Experience had taught him that most of the inhabitants were in some way untouchable. If they were not personally influential, they had important friends and threatened to complain, as Prieur had complained, directly to the Minister of the Interior.

Janvier had slowed down. The car had almost come to a halt. The Superintendent muttered:

"The bitch!"

Then, aware of his helplessness, in a resigned, bitter tone:

"Go ahead . . . To the Quai . . ."

To the Quai des Orfèvres, where he had the right to pester anyone with questions for twenty-four hours on end, even for two or three days, with intervals for glasses of beer and sandwiches, for short rests on a mattress. Anyone except for people like that, except for Nicole Prieur.

Janvier said nothing, knowing that this was no time to speak.

"A girl of that class must go abroad," said Maigret suddenly. "So she's got a passport. Which means a card with her photograph at Police Headquarters."

He was well acquainted with the office where these cards were filed in green metal cabinets, and on hundreds of occasions he had consulted the official who kept the files up to date, a certain Loriot, who never hesitated to let Maigret look in the drawers.

But not for Mademoiselle Prieur! He had to go about it another way. Aline was right: he needed a photograph of the girl as soon as possible.

"Has Barnacle still got his Leica?"

"He'd rather leave his wife than his camera."

"Has he got a wife?"

An odd thing: Maigret had known Barnacle for over thirty years and had never known anything about his private life.

He thought he was a bachelor. In his loose black suit, with shiny elbows and tattered cuffs, which he had worn for years and which was always missing a button, Barnacle, looking as though he were stooping under the weight of adversity, seemed more like a widower still in mourning.

He was working at the Quai when Maigret first arrived. Maigret had called him "Monsieur Barnacle" and had continued to do so. So the detectives, too, said "Monsieur Barnacle," with a note of irony, as though "Monsieur" were a Christian name or a nickname.

In his office he rang for the old messenger.

"Send Monsieur Barnacle in to me if he's in the building."

The noise had died down in the offices and the corridors. It was almost six o'clock. The sun was still high, and as yet there was no breeze; the curtains, on either side of the windows, were hanging without a tremor.

"Did you want me, sir?"

"Sit down, Monsieur Barnacle."

The detective was only two and a half years older than he was. Would Maigret in two and a half years have that resigned expression, those mirthless, indifferent eyes, that flabby, worn skin, those tired shoulders?

Hadn't Barnacle always been like that? He was married, so he must have been more or less in love. He had courted a girl, offered her violets, had walked arm in arm with her, stopping to kiss her. It was almost unbelievable.

"Not only is he married," Janvier had told him, "but in the neighborhood his wife is supposed to be pretty fast. She often comes home late; sometimes she doesn't come home all night, and it's he who has to cook the dinner and clean the house after the day's work. . . ."

Barnacle was no great brain but, once on a trail, he stuck to it and remained as inconspicuous in a crowd as certain gray walls in Paris covered with tattered advertisements.

"I'd like to give you an assignment, Monsieur Barnacle, but I hesitate to because if there were any word of it, in higher circles, you might be made to retire before your time."

"That would mean only three months less trailing around Paris."

There was no reproach in his voice. Barnacle wasn't embittered, didn't resent anyone; he probably didn't resent his wife either.

"I'll carry out your assignment, sir."

"It means photographing a girl. . . . I don't know where, when or how, and that'll be your problem."

"I'm used to that."

It was true. Recourse was often had to Barnacle's talents as a photographer and his dingy appearance. When the photograph of a suspect was needed, he would stand anywhere the suspect might go and, his Leica hanging from his neck, pretend to be one of the strolling photographers becoming increasingly common on the Champs-Elysées, the big boulevards and everywhere in Paris.

Like them, he even had little cards printed, with a fictitious name, address and telephone number, which he pressed into the hands of passers-by.

"She lives on Boulevard de Courcelles and goes to lectures at the Sorbonne. She has a friend on Boulevard Saint-Germain, the daughter of Doctor Bouet, whose number you'll find in the directory. Apart from that I don't know whom she sees or where she spends her time."

"Has she got a car?"

"If she has, it's recent, because she's only eighteen. Her uncle is a big shot, Head of Petitions at the State Council, and I suppose he has a car and a chauffeur. . . . I warn you that if you ask the hall porter he'll inform the Commissioner's office at once. The Commissioner has strictly forbidden us to do anything about her. . . . Have you got the picture?"

"That'll take slightly longer. . . . Can you tell me what she looks like?"

Maigret gave him the description of Nicole Prieur.

"In this weather," said Monsieur Barnacle to himself, "there's a chance that she hasn't spent the afternoon at home. People like that dine late. . . . I might still have time. . . ."

At the door he turned around with something resembling a smile on his gray face.

"If there's any trouble, don't put yourself out for me. . . . For a long time I've wanted to tell them to go to hell!"

Maigret couldn't get over it. The resigned sheep that

Barnacle had always been proved, three months before retirement, to be a ferocious sheep. He added with a snigger:

"They have no right to touch my pension. . . . They owe it to me, you see? . . . It's my money, money they've kept for me all these years."

Maigret signed the papers on his desk. Nothing new could be done without the photograph. He felt empty, useless.

And yet, out of habit, as he had done every evening before leaving the Police Judiciare, he pushed open the door of the detectives' room. Lucas was there, his head balder than when he had entered the Superintendent's service.

"Come in a minute . . ."

He was angry with himself for not telling him. It wasn't because of the Commissioner's orders, since he'd told Janvier, but because he didn't have the courage to tell that humiliating story all over again.

"Come in . . . Sit down if you like."

"Something wrong, chief?"

"Yes . . . It doesn't matter. . . . You don't by any chance know anyone who goes to lectures at the Sorbonne, do you?"

"Lectures on what?"

"I don't know."

"You know, there are thousands of students. . . ."

Lucas looked at the carpet contemplatively.

"I know one of the porters quite well—he's a distant relation of my wife, but he's only a porter. . . ."

"Are you on good terms with each other?"

"I see him every three or four years at a family reunion, a funeral or a marriage."

"Can you call him and arrange to meet him somewhere? . . . In a café, for example?"

"I'll see if he's on duty."

"Call from here."

The distant cousin of Madame Lucas was named Oscar Coutant, and he finally came to the telephone.

"Lucas, yes . . . How are you? . . . No . . . She's very well. . . . She sends her regards. . . . Aunt Emma? . . . We haven't seen her for at least three months. . . . Just as deaf as ever, yes . . . Say . . . I'd like to meet you and ask you something. . . . Nothing important . . . I'd rather not be seen down there. . . . What? . . . Half past six? . . . That'll give me time to get there. . . . The first on the left, coming from Boulevard Saint-Michel? . . . I'll be there."

Lucas gave Maigret a questioning glance.

"All right . . . See you then."

And to the Superintendent:

"We got him just as he was leaving. He'll be expecting us in a bar on Rue Monsieur-le-Prince where he always goes for an apéritif. . . . It's on his way. . . . What shall I ask him?"

"I'd better go with you. Quick, call a taxi."

"Except for a little wine at meals . . ." Pardon had ordered.

How many bars had Maigret been obliged to go to in twenty-four hours? He could have ordered fruit juice, of course. . . .

At the age of forty Oscar Coutant had the soft contours of men who sit motionless all day and have a tendency to drink apéritifs. He was obviously proud of his job, which he must have performed with dignity if not with solemnity. He worked at the Sorbonne. Illustrious professors shook his hand as they went by. Students whom he didn't hesitate to scold when necessary had well-known names and would one day become bankers or politicians.

"This is Superintendent Maigret, my chief."

"Pleased to meet you . . . I've never seen you with us before."

He obviously meant the Sorbonne, not his apartment.

"At your service, Superintendent. One always likes meeting celebrities. And you certainly are a celebrity! . . . I imagined you fatter, if you don't mind my saying so. Fatter and taller . . . We must be about the same size, and yet I weigh over 160 pounds. . . . What'll you have? . . . Some anisette? . . . Jules! The same again for me and two anisettes for these gentlemen . . . So you're interested in one of our kids?"

"I wonder if you know a student named Nicole Prieur. . . ."

"The niece of . . ."

"Yes."

"That's the Etoile group, kids who give us plenty of trouble and whom we have to be strict with. . . . There are about twenty of them, boys and girls, who turn up in sports cars . . . Jaguars or Ferraris; I don't know— and park them in the spaces reserved for the professors. . . . Luckily some of the professors don't have cars and usually take the métro. . . ."

"What does she study?"

"Just let me get it straight . . . We've got it all written out, you see, but there are so many names to remember. . . ."

From what he said one would have thought he bore

the whole weight of the Sorbonne on his shoulders.

"Good . . . I remember now. . . . She takes history of art, with a friend, the daughter of a doctor, Bouet. . . ."

"Who else is in the Etoile group?"

"That's what we call it because most of them live near the Arc de Triomphe, on Avenue Hoche, Avenue Marceau, Avenue Foch, and so on. . . . The craziest of all is the son of a South American ambassador, who drives an open blue Ferrari. . . . He's named Martinez and he's always with a group of girls. . . . Another one, a tall, fair boy, is the son of Dariman, of the chemical company. . . . You know, the group isn't always the same. They quarrel. . . . You see new ones. . . . In the evening and most of the night they meet in a club."

"Do you know where?"

"It was mentioned in the papers. . . . Of course, I don't go to those places and I don't really know about them. . . . It's on Avenue de la Grande-Armée, or near there. . . . In the restaurant on the ground floor, anybody who can afford to can go for a meal. The club is in the basement, and you have apparently to be a member to get in. . . . Just a minute . . . I'm trying to remember the name. . . . It's on the tip of my tongue."

"The Hundred Keys?" suggested Lucas.

"That's it. . . . How did you know?"

"Because, like you, I read about it in the papers. . . Once you're a member, you're given a symbolic key, a golden key, which is supposed to open the door of the club. . . ."

Maigret got up. The cousin was actually about to order another round and make some interminable observations about the Sorbonne.

"Thank you, and please excuse me."

A little later, on Boulevard Saint-Michel, he sank into the seat of a taxi and said:

"Boulevard Richard-Lenoir."

"Very well, Superintendent."

The Chief Commissioner of Police would soon forbid the taxi drivers to recognize him!

He had rarely been so eager to get home and meet the tender, gay eyes of his wife.

5

As soon as she heard his steps on the stairs she went to open the door, in her flower-patterned housecoat and slippers. The apartment smelled of floor polish.

"I'm sorry I'm not dressed, but when they called to tell me you weren't coming home for lunch, I thought you were on a new case so I decided to polish the floor. What's the matter? Are you worried?"

"I'm on a new case, as you say. The case of Maigret."

He gave a rather sickly smile, because it's distressing toward the end of a career such as his to see that your boss distrusts you, particularly when your boss is a conceited young peacock, seething with ambition, like the Commissioner.

If the morning's indignation had vanished, there remained nevertheless an underlying bitterness that the Superintendent had made every effort to conceal from his colleagues, from good old Janvier and Lucas in particular.

"We might be at Meung-sur-Loire sooner than we think."

"What are you talking about?"

"What happened last night . That girl who called and whom I went to meet on Rue de Seine."

"Don't tell me she was found dead."

"For me it's almost worse. She got home at eight in the morning. She lives on Boulevard de Courcelles, and her uncle is one of the leading men in the country."

"That's odd. I've been thinking all day about that girl and what she told you. Something was worrying me. . . ."

"She's accusing me of having picked her up in a café where she'd gone to call a friend and of having tried to seduce her after promising to let her watch an arrest. I supposedly took advantage of her innocence, made her drunk, dragged her from bar to bar, and carried her almost unconscious into a hotel room, where I undressed her by force."

"Who believed that?"

"Apparently all those top gentlemen, starting with the Minister of the Interior and going on to the Commissioner of Police."

"Have you resigned?"

"Not yet."

"I hope you're going to defend yourself."

"I've been trying to, since eleven o'clock this morning. . . . That's partly why I'm going to take you out to dinner."

"It's a good time. Since I didn't know when you were coming home, I've only got a cold dinner. . . . What shall I wear?"

"Your best dress."

A few minutes later, under the shower, he tried to hear what his wife was saying. They had to talk at the tops of their voices.

"Have you questioned the girl?"

"I'm not allowed to go near her or her house."

"Why did she do it? Have you any idea?"

"Not yet . . . I might have one this evening."

As they dressed they said comforting things to each other. Madame Maigret had kept her head and had been the first to mention resigning. She hadn't mistrusted her husband for a moment and had retained her good humor.

"Where are we going?"

"To a restaurant that gets two stars from the Guide Bleue, on Avenue de la Grande-Armée."

They were the longest days of the year. The sun hadn't set, and Paris still kept her windows open to the cool evening air. Men in shirt sleeves smoked their pipes or cigarettes as they watched the passers-by; women in nightgowns called to each other from window to window. Walking along the streets, one could hear the discordant sound of radios.

They went into the métro. His colleagues teased Maigret about this. He was one of the few men at the Quai not to have a car. This was partly due to the fact that when he was old enough to learn to drive and enjoy it he couldn't afford it. Now it was too late. He might start staring at the sun playing on the leaves of the trees and run over somebody, or, during a case, plunge into a brown study.

He thought about it ironically, sitting next to his wife in the métro, swinging with her and the other passengers from left to right, and from right to left, forward and backward, backward and forward.

Madame Maigret could have driven him. Many men are driven around by their wives.

"Can you imagine me responsible for a ton of iron hurtling along at seventy miles per hour? I'd be so frightened of hurting someone! . . . Especially with the policemen making one drive faster . . ."

Janvier had a small car. Lucas was thinking of getting one. Maigret would have to when he lived at Meung-sur-Loire, unless he and his wife were to live like a provincial couple of 1900. In the country he might get used to it, without being frightened of mistaking the traffic lights for children's balloons. All he'd have to do would be to come to Paris by train as he used to.

"What are you thinking about?"

"Nothing . . ."

Nothing and everything, his life, his career, the morning's interview in the Commissioner's office, Manuel in his wheelchair, and what a strange girl Aline was.

The restaurant, its unobtrusive windows covered with tulle, was almost at the end of the street. It was comfortable and elegant, half empty because most of its clients had already gone to the country or the seaside. At the right of the entrance a staircase led down to the basement, where a large red curtain was hung.

"Would you like a table near one of the windows?"

"Here."

Maigret pointed to one opposite the stairs, let his wife sit by the window, and studied the menu.

"D'you want canard à l'orange?"

"What else is there?"

"A whole page . . ."

They finally chose some cooling vichyssoise and the duck, which was the plat du jour. The headwaiter had joined the other waiters and must have been whispering to them:

"That's Superintendent Maigret. . . ."

They all looked at him with curiosity. He was used to it, but, despite the Commissioner's opinion, it was hardly pleasant.

"Was there a special reason for choosing this restaurant? We've never been here before."

"I have, a long time ago, during some investigation. . . . As far as I can remember, I was looking for an international crook who used to dine here."

"It seems respectable."

"International crooks always eat in respectable restaurants and stay in the best hotels."

It was nine o'clock. A young woman came in and went downstairs. She looked more like a coatroom or ladies' room attendant than a client.

Ten minutes later it was a tired-looking man. He wasn't part of the gilded youth either, but was on the wrong side of the fence, on the side of those who serve the others.

The club downstairs was going to open later, and the staff was getting it ready, as they do small bars and cafés in the morning.

Muffled by the curtain a few notes could be heard, followed by others in different keys; they were trying out the records to regulate the sound.

"Do you think it's better than mine?"

"No . . . Nothing in a restaurant is better than at home."

She meant the duck. They chatted about everything and nothing. Occasionally, when she felt he wasn't looking, Madame Maigret looked solemnly at her husband, trying to fathom exactly how deeply he had been affected. He'd ordered a bottle of vintage Saint-Emilion, which she hardly touched.

Did she also wonder whether he was drinking too much and whether that wasn't one of the reasons for his being tired? Because he did look tired. She had mentioned it for a brief instant to Pardon, in a whisper. Her husband had overheard her. What had the doctor replied?

"Some cheese? There's some very tempting-looking Brie."

"I'll have a little bit."

"Waiter . . . the club in the basement . . ."

"Yes, sir . . . the Hundred Keys . . ."

"Why a hundred?"

"I wouldn't know that. . . . I'm in charge of the restaurant, not the club."

"Can anyone go in?"

"No. It's strictly private. One has to be a member."

"How does one join?"

"Do you really want to join it?"

He seemed surprised and looked alternately at the Superintendent and Madame Maigret, who blushed.

"Are you surprised?"

"No . . . Yes . . . It's mainly a club for young people who come to dance. . . . They'll soon be coming. . . . Shall I call the organizer?"

He was already on his way down to the basement, where he stayed for some time before returning with a young man in a dinner jacket whom Maigret thought he recognized.

"This is Monsieur Landry, who'll give you all the details."

The young man held out his hand.

"Good evening, Superintendent."

He bowed to Madame Maigret.

"Delighted to meet you . . . Not many people have the chance of meeting you, because your husband doesn't seem to like taking you out in public. . . . May I?"

He pulled out a chair, sat down, took a silver cigarette case out of his pocket.

"Do you mind if I smoke?"

He was about thirty-five. His dinner jacket was perfectly cut, and he wore it with the ease of those who dress every evening.

A good-looking boy, he could be accused of too much self-assurance, of a sly, almost aggressive expression. His smile was charming, but one felt that at the slightest threat he would unsheathe his claws.

"I hear you're interested in our club?"

"I'd like to become a member. . . . Unless there's an age limit?"

"We thought of having one at the beginning. . . . We thought of thirty, but that would have excluded some excellent people. . . . Have you heard of the Hundred Keys, Superintendent?"

"Vaguely, and I'm rather surprised to find you here. . . . I hear you're the organizer."

"Secretary, organizer, everything really . . . The word 'organizer' is in fashion."

Maigret had known him when Landry couldn't have been more than eighteen. He had just come from the provinces. His father was postmaster general at Angers, or Tours—anyhow, in one of those large towns on the Loire. Eager to get ahead in Parisian life, he wrote for gossip columns, sneaking skillfully into the mass of receptions and cocktail parties where he could talk to celebrities.

One day he had come to see Maigret at the Quai des Orfèvres, full of assurance, showing the press card of a weekly magazine specializing in scandal.

Marcel Landry was not afraid of anybody, particularly not the Superintendent.

"You see, Superintendent, what interests our readers isn't the organization of the Police Judiciare, which the daily papers often write about, but seeing behind the scenes in an organization that deals with all the so-called dirty linen of Paris. . . .

"I hope the expression doesn't shock you. . . . Of course it doesn't mean printing names. . . . And I can add that my paper would pay a high price. . . ."

At the time he had been too young for Maigret to be angry, and the Superintendent had shown him the door as politely as possible. Two or three years later he had heard his voice on the radio, where he had become a commercial announcer.

Then there'd been a gap. Landry was one of those people you meet everywhere for a while, whom you get used to greeting without knowing who they are, who suddenly disappear for no apparent reason and who crop up again in a different guise.

What obscure jobs had Landry done all these years? If he'd broken the law, the police hadn't heard about it.

He'd cropped up again as secretary to a singer, who used him as her gentleman-in-waiting.

After leaving her two or three years later, he had written memoirs revealing every detail of the private life of the singer, who had then sued him.

Maigret didn't know whether she had won or lost the case, and now, in front of him, both smiling and nervous, was the young man he used to know, sixteen or seventeen years older, but still remarkably well preserved.

"The Hundred Keys, you see, is different from the clubs that open every week in Paris, because it's a real club. One really has to be a member to pass through the red curtain to the basement. As for the figure a hundred, that's to limit the number of members, which, incidentally, is now only eighty-five or eighty-six."

"Boys and girls belonging to rich families, I suppose?"

"For purposes of selection we have set the initiation fee at six hundred francs. . . . On the other hand, the charge for drinks is only just over the cost. . . . Do you dance?"

Maigret was so astonished that he didn't immediately understand the meaning of the question.

"What did you say?"

"I asked if you liked dancing, modern dancing, of course, because you can't expect to dance waltzes or polkas here. . . . Do you dance, too, Madame Maigret?"

Not knowing what to answer, she looked to her husband for help.

"Yes! . . . We both dance. . . . Does that surprise you?"

"Slightly . . . I've never seen you on the dance floor, and you have the reputation of being . . ."

"An old fogey who puffs at his pipe and looks sulky . . ."

"I didn't say that. . . . Do you seriously want to become a member?"

"Seriously."

"Do you know two club members to back you? This also proves it's a real club. Every candidate has to have two backers, and a committee of twelve members votes whether or not to admit him."

"If I could have a look at the membership list, I'd certainly find more than two people to back me."

Marcel Landry didn't flinch. They both knew they were acting. Landry gave the Superintendent a sharp look, more intrigued than worried, smiled again and went toward the stairs. When he returned, he held a register bound in red leather.

"This book is always at the disposal of the members, on a table behind the curtain. As you will see, it contains not only the names and addresses of the members, but also those of every member's backers. . . .

"I'd be surprised if you came across any of your clients.

"Under A: Abouchère, the son of Senator Abouchère . . . Viscomte d'Arceau . . . He doesn't use his title here. His father's a member of the Jockey Club, and he'll be a member of it, too, someday, just like his grandfather and his grandfather's father. . . . Barillard, of the Barillard Oil Company . . . Next month Mademoiselle Barillard is going to marry Eric Cornal, of

Cornal Biscuits, whom she met here. . . . This register could be considered the young people's social directory.

"Some of them are studying, and we don't see much of them at the moment, because they're taking their exams. . . . Others are working. . . . We've also got some married couples."

The addresses were all what are known as good addresses, addresses that would place one financially.

Maigret let his finger glide down the page, moving his lips. His finger stopped by a name:

"François Mélan, 38, stomatologist, 32b Rue des Acacias."

"Isn't that the dentist who lives in a private house?"

"I must confess I've never been to see him. He comes here frequently, although he hardly ever dances. It seems he's a remarkably intelligent man. . . ."

His finger continued, stopped again as Maigret made every effort to conceal his interest.

"Nicole Prieur, 17, 42 Boulevard de Courcelles . . ."

The most interesting thing of all was farther on, in the backers' section. For Nicole, the backers were none other than Dr. François Mélan and Martine Bouet.

"Isn't Mademoiselle Bouet a tall, blonde girl?"

"I see you know her. She's one of the best dancers in the club. A great friend of Mademoiselle Prieur . . ."

"Does Mademoiselle Prieur come often?"

Landry's fingers tapped the table. He may have had a clear conscience, but in the indecisive career he had chosen, and with his ambitions, it wasn't wise for him to be on the wrong side of the police.

The Commissioner's instructions hadn't yet reached

Avenue de la Grande-Armée. As for Madame Maigret, she looked on with curiosity at what her husband was doing. It was the first time she had been able to, and she tried to guess what lay hidden beneath the seemingly commonplace remarks of the two men.

"Mademoiselle Prieur is one of our most regular clients. . . . She comes at least two or three times a week."

"Alone?"

"Alone or with a party."

"Does she stay until closing time?"

"Quite often."

"What time do you close?"

"That depends on who's there. Sometimes members bring a stage or movie star, a singer, some celebrity. . . . On occasion we've closed at six in the morning, but usually everybody's left by two or three o'clock."

"Has Mademoiselle Prieur ever come with her uncle?"

"Once, at the beginning. With most girls it's almost a tradition. On the first evening the parents want to find out for themselves. . . . Monsieur Prieur surprised us all. We expected someone rather solemn. . . . Do you know him?"

"No."

"He's Head of Petitions at the State Council and said to be one of our most able jurists. . . . Well, he's about fifty or fifty-five, with broad shoulders, the features of a peasant, a short, thick beard and bushy eyebrows. . . . He's like a sprightly old boar. . . . He ordered a double whisky. . . . Within a quarter of an hour he was on the floor dancing with his niece. . . . He stayed for two hours, and on his way out he congratulated me and added that if he hadn't got into the habit of getting up very early, he'd have stayed longer."

"One gets wrong ideas about people. . . . Did he come back?"

"No."

"Not last night either?"

"Certainly not."

"Who was Mademoiselle Prieur with last night?"

"Last night? . . . Just a minute . . . I have to visualize the tables. . . . I didn't see her last night. . . ."

"Nor her friend?"

"You mean Martine Bouet? . . . No . . . I can't remember her."

"Thank you."

"Do you still want to join? . . . Have you found some possible backers on this list? . . ."

"There are plenty of them. . . . I'll think about it. . . . I see your members are arriving."

"Yes, I ought to go down."

"Incidentally, do you know Manuel?"

"The actor?"

"Manuel Palmari."

"What does he do?"

"Nothing."

"I can't quite see . . . No . . . Should I know him?"

"Better not . . . Thank you again, Monsieur Landry."

"Don't you want to have a look downstairs? . . . Don't you either, Madame Maigret? . . . In that case, if you'll excuse me . . ."

Madame Maigret patiently waited for her husband to pay the bill. When they were outside she asked:

"Did you find out what you wanted?"

"I found out a lot of things but I don't know how important they are. . . . While we're in the area, let's walk by Rue des Acacias."

On the way he sighed and said:

"As long as Nicole Prieur doesn't decide to go dancing at the club tonight . . ."

"Do you think he'll talk?"

"He'll certainly warn her and tell her I questioned him insistently about her. . . . If she repeats it to her uncle, we can start packing tomorrow."

He said that so lightly that she asked, squeezing his arm tighter:

"Are you sad? Are you trying to hide it?"

"No. You see, at this point I wonder whether I'd rather quit or carry on. . . ."

"Was the shock very violent this morning?"

"Quite . . . For the first time in my life I was on the wrong side of the desk. . . . I wonder if I'll have the guts to go on investigating. . . ."

"Why didn't you defend yourself?"

"Because it wouldn't have done any good and I might have lost my temper."

"Do you think this girl . . ."

"She doesn't count. She's just a pawn. . . . It's all too well worked out, including the question of time and the two possible testimonies. . . . First Martine Bouet . . . the token for the telephone . . . just one . . . Then Désiré . . . She certainly didn't reel in front of him and didn't talk to him as though she were drunk. She spoke to me in a whisper, and he couldn't hear her. . . . The bars where I'm supposed to have made her drunk . . .

"The descriptions she gave could apply to fifty bars and night clubs in Saint-Germain-des-Prés, and in at least a dozen of these places the crowd is thick enough for us to have passed unnoticed. . . .

"Finally, the hotel, where I did indeed go up to the second floor with her and where she was clever enough to keep me in her room for a good ten minutes . . ."

"Have you got an idea?"

"Fragments . . . masses of fragments . . . Unfortunately, only one of these fragments is the right one, and one has to choose carefully. . . ."

Rue des Acacias was almost empty. Lights were still on in some of the windows, including two of the windows of the dentist's house. Maigret went up to the nameplate he'd seen only in the distance, when he went to visit Manuel. "Doctor François Mélan, stomatologist. From 10:00 to 12:00 and by appointment."

"Why does he put stomatologist?"

"It's more distinguished than dentist."

He looked up at Manuel's windows and saw Aline, leaning against the window sill, smoking a cigarette.

A few yards farther on a man standing in a doorway murmured, as Maigret and his wife went by:

"Good night, sir."

It was Jaquemain, one of his detectives, who was going to spend the night on the street.

"Good night, dear fellow."

The couple took the métro at the Ternes station. The day had been depressing but ended, thanks to Madame Maigret, in relative serenity. Over Boulevard Richard-Lenoir a large moon dyed pink watched them walk toward their house arm in arm.

A traffic accident held up his bus, and he arrived at the Quai des Orfèvres at ten past nine.

"Has anyone asked for me?"

"No, sir . . . Only Lourtie."

"I'll see him after the report."

He took the papers on his desk and rushed to the Chief's office, where the other superintendents had already gathered.

"I'm sorry, sir. . . ."

"Go on, Bernard."

The head of the Gambling Squad continued his report in a monotone.

"Good . . . And you, Maigret? . . . Another jeweler's yesterday . . ."

Maigret had expected a distressing session, with evasive and reproachful glances, but it didn't look as though anything that had taken place in the Chief Commissioner's office the day before had leaked out.

The morning routine. The windows open. The birds singing. A tramp on the bank of the Seine industriously doing his washing.

A quarter of an hour later Barnacle, still dressed in black, slipped into Maigret's office.

"I've got three of them," he announced, handing Maigret some enlarged photographs, "but I don't know which the right one is."

He meant the right girl, Nicole Prieur. The first, a chubby girl with simple eyes, bore no resemblance to her. The second was just sixteen, which made one think that poor Barnacle's knowledge of girls was still pretty rudimentary.

The third was indeed Nicole, wearing a light dress, with a white handbag under her arm.

"I've got another picture of her, standing up."

Like a conjurer, the detective drew it out of a pocket

of his loose jacket. The photograph had been taken by the railings of Parc Monceau, where the girl held a dachshund on a leash as it lifted its leg.

"Is that what you wanted?"

"Perfect, Barnacle."

"D'you want any more copies?"

"If possible. Three or four . . ."

It didn't matter so much any more. Without Oscar, the distant cousin of Lucas, or, rather, of Madame Lucas, these photographs would have played a more important part. They might still play one, although the Superintendent thought he had a clue.

"Do you want to have them printed at once?"

Maigret was forgetting that the detective had risked his job by taking these photographs in secret.

"Did you have any trouble?"

"Not much . . . You know, I'm not conspicuous in the street. I sink into the landscape. . . . In the squares and parks there are always a couple of fellows looking like me, and people don't notice them. . . ."

He spoke about himself with neither bitterness nor irony.

"She didn't notice anything. She was concentrating on her dog, which wouldn't cross the street, so she had to carry it. I've got a shot of her carrying the dog, but it's out of focus, so I didn't develop it."

"Thanks, Barnacle . . . That was good of you."

"You've always been good to me."

When Barnacle left, it was Janvier's turn.

"Is it the girl you wanted?"

"Yes. I'd like you to go to Rue Fontaine. . . ."

"To the Clou Doré?"

"Yes. Show the waiters the photograph. Try to find

out if they've ever seen her at the restaurant. You might drift around the neighborhood, too."

"Aren't you going out, chief?"

"Yes. I'm going to Rue des Acacias."

"Don't you want me to drive you there?"

"I'd rather you went to Montmartre before the rush hour. Tell Lucas to wait for me downstairs with a car. . . ."

There was already that hot steam in the air that one sees over the sea, and the Champs-Elysées shimmered in the golden light.

"Thanks for the cousin, Lucas."

"Not at all, chief. He's cost me quite a hangover. He was so proud to have met you and had a drink with you that we had one anisette after the other. From now on he'll talk about his friend Maigret as though you'd been to school together. Where shall I drop you? . . . At Manuel's?"

It had become a habit.

"If you like. I'm going to the house opposite."

"Shall I wait for you?"

"Yes. It might be very brief."

He rang the bell. A Spanish-looking woman with a long face glared at him disagreeably and asked:

"What d'you want?"

"To see the doctor."

"Have you got an appointment?"

"Yes."

"Go up then . . . The door on the right . . ."

She watched him as he went up the old oak steps, which were partly covered with stained greenish velvet. The maid's apron was stained, too. Madame Maigret would have thought the house badly kept.

6

He took his time, so as to keep the maid hanging around on the ground floor. And, on his way upstairs, he tried to define the smell that pervaded the house, a smell he knew, not lacking charm, which dated from his childhood: the smell of old houses, and damp woodwork with a tang of mold.

At the back the little house must have kept one of those gardens one still occasionally finds in Paris, with a tree that, judging from its smell, Maigret would have sworn to be a lime.

He had never been in such a dubious position before, because he had no right to be here and, on the slightest complaint from the dentist, the Superintendent would be disowned and have a lot to explain.

It almost looked as though he were accumulating all the faults of which the Commissioner had accused him.

Hardly had his liking for informers been mentioned when he rushed to see Manuel, who was one.

He was forbidden to talk to Nicole and he went to a bar to question a member of the staff at the Sorbonne about her.

He was forbidden to make any mention of the matter at the Police Judiciare, so he first told Janvier about it, and then Lucas, and sent poor Barnacle to photograph the young lady in secret.

Finally, on such a thin pretext that Marcel Landry had not been deceived for a second, he had asked to see the register of a private club to which the niece of the Head of Petitions belonged.

All these crimes in one day! After having gone so far, he didn't see why he should stop. Either he succeeded or else he failed and, in everybody's eyes, his career would end disastrously.

Had he at least discovered something? Yes. He wasn't yet sure of the value of the discovery but he had found a link between two women as different from each other and living in circumstances as opposed to one another's as Nicole Prieur and Manuel's mistress, Aline. Nicole had been backed by Doctor Mélan at the Hundred Keys. And, on at least one occasion the day before, Aline had been to the same doctor to have her teeth looked at.

All this crossed his mind in a few seconds, and on the first floor he didn't go to the door on the right, as the Spanish woman had said, but to the door on the left. He quite liked to see the interiors of the houses of the people he was dealing with, especially the rooms to which he wasn't invited.

The door was either locked or bolted, and below him a voice said:

"Don't you know your right from your left?"

The maid had come up a few steps. Her large black eyes had about as much expression as a cow's in a meadow, but nevertheless she was a handsome woman.

Written on an enamel plate was RING AND ENTER.

He rang, turned the knob and found himself in a waiting room looking like a provincial drawing room where a single person was sitting, a youngish woman who seemed anxious and ill.

Ignoring the magazines piled on a gilded table, she sat motionless, her hands on her bag, staring at the flower-patterned carpet. She barely gave him an indifferent glance before returning to her melancholy contemplation.

A door opened opposite him, and the secretary, a nurse with a long nose, whom Aline had spoken about, addressed him unpleasantly. Her voice was dry, her eyes hard. She was an ugly woman, ugly enough not to have known youth or adolescence and to hold the whole world responsible for it.

"What do you want?"

"To see Dr. Mélan."

"For a consultation?"

"Yes."

"Have you got an appointment?"

"No."

"The doctor sees patients by appointment only."

"But the plate on the right of the door says that he sees patients from ten to twelve and in the afternoon by appointment only."

"It's an old plate."

"Last night I had a violent toothache, and aspirin didn't relieve the pain. I'd like the doctor . . . ."

"Have you been here before?"

"No."

"Do you live in the area?"

"No."

"Why did you choose Dr. Mélan?"

"I was passing by and I saw his plate . . ."

"Follow me."

She showed him into a little office with white walls, but of a white as dubious as the rest of the house. She sat at the desk.

"Sit down . . . I can't guarantee that the doctor'll be able to see you between patients, but I'll fill in your card just in case. What's your name?"

"Maigret . . . Jules Maigret."

"Occupation?"

"Civil servant."

"Age and address?"

"Fifty-two . . . Boulevard Richard-Lenoir."

She didn't flinch. Admittedly her head was bent over the card and he couldn't see her eyes.

"Which tooth is hurting you?"

"A right molar. I don't know which one—the second, I suppose."

"Wait next door . . . I can't guarantee anything. . . . If you're in a hurry, I suggest you try another dentist."

"I'll wait."

The window of the waiting room did indeed look out on the garden, and, in the middle of a lawn parched by the heat, he saw the lime tree he thought would be there.

He could also see a dilapidated greenhouse against a fairly high wall, some garden tools and some badly kept flower beds.

Beyond the garden stood a house of six or seven floors. It was the back that he saw, and out of several windows washing was drying on lines.

He sat down and fiddled with his pipe in his pocket. He might have lit it had it not been for the sad-looking woman sitting opposite him. A clock ticked, a black marble clock like the ones in the offices at the Quai des Orfèvres. It said twenty minutes past ten. He wondered if he would still be waiting when it said twelve.

He tried not to think, not to formulate theories; to keep his mind free and to pass the time, he took in minute details: the mirror over the mantelpiece, where flies had for years left little brown marks, the Second Empire andirons and the odd chairs. Nothing was ugly in itself. Not even the house, built around 1870 or 1880, well before the apartment houses on the same street.

It would soon disappear. One could feel that the end was near and that that was possibly why the owner wouldn't go to the expense of repainting it.

There was also the feeling of a house without a woman, without children.

The third door of the room was padded, like the doors of old notaries and some offices. Nothing could be heard of what was going on on the other side.

The whole building was silent, too, and if the window were shut one could hardly hear the birds sing in the lime tree.

Outside it was hot. Here one was struck by the cold.

"The doctor apologizes, miss. . . . He'll see you in a few minutes."

It was the nurse, to whom the young patient replied with a look of resignation.

"Please follow me, Monsieur Maigret."

She opened the padded door, then the gray door behind it. They suddenly passed from the dark into the sunlight. A man in white, sitting at a Louis-Philippe desk, was holding the card that had just been filled in in the Superintendent's name.

The nurse had disappeared. François Mélan took his time reading the card through as the Superintendent came two or three steps nearer.

"Sit down."

He was very different from what one would have gathered from Marcel Landry's conversation, and it was even harder to visualize him than Nicole's uncle in the basement of the Hundred Keys, throbbing with music.

He was a proper redhead, with hair of that flaming red which would have earned him, during his childhood, the nickname "Carrot Head." He looked up, and behind thick glasses with no apparent rims shone clear blue eyes.

He looked very young, and at the age of thirty-eight he could still be taken for a student.

"Did you have this toothache suddenly?"

He made no allusion to Maigret's profession. And his face betrayed no curiosity.

"Last night, yes, just as I was going to bed."

"Have you had any trouble before? During the last weeks?"

"No. I've got pretty good teeth. I've only been to the dentist about ten times in my life."

"Let's have a look."

He got up, and Maigret made a new discovery. Mélan was huge, almost a head taller than he was. His smock, hardly cleaner than the nurse's, didn't reach down to his knees, and his trousers needed pressing.

The adjustable chair was in the middle of the room with, above it, the usual lamp disk the color of a full moon. Between the chair and the window, instruments lay on a narrow table.

Maigret sat down hesitantly. A chain was fastened around his neck and a bib attached to it. Pressing his foot on the pedal the doctor gradually raised the chair.

All this was quite normal. The same scene, with the same movements, was taking place at the same time at hundreds of Parisian dentists'.

"Put your head back . . . Good . . . Open your mouth . . ."

Here the silence was less intense than in the rest of the house. The room looked onto the road. Instead of frosted glass, the window had net curtains, through which one could see the cream-colored façade opposite, open windows, a woman walking to and fro in her kitchen.

The noises of the street drifted up—a vague din with a few sharper sounds.

Mélan impassively passed a little mirror over a flame and took up a shiny instrument.

"Open wider, please . . ."

As he bent over, Maigret saw his face very close, as though through a magnifying glass. The skin was thick, reddish, and, as with many redheads, granular, with a few freckles.

The doctor didn't say a word. Since the Superintendent had come in, he had spoken as little as possible and, when he got up and stretched out his large body, he moved with the clumsiness of a shy man.

With a pointed instrument he scraped the surface of the molars.

"Can you feel anything?"

"No," Maigret tried to say, his mouth wide open.

"And now?"

"No."

"Here?"

Nothing. It was true. Maigret had hardly ever had anything wrong with his teeth. The doctor exchanged his instruments for a little hammer.

"Does this hurt?"

"It's unpleasant."

"But no sharp pain?"

Why did the Superintendent suddenly swear not to have an injection under any circumstances? He started to feel fear. Not panic. A vague, indeterminate fear. He found himself practically horizontal, his head back, his mouth open, in a chair in which he was in some way imprisoned.

Why had he come into this house? Because he was looking for the man who had attacked him viciously. The word Pardon used when he asked him:

"In all your career have you ever come across a really wicked, vicious criminal?"

He was looking for someone who, either to get rid of him or because he hated him, had tried to dishonor him by hatching an intricate plot, worked out to the last detail, using as an instrument a girl of good family. Why in fact does one say "good" family? Is it because all the others are of "bad" family?

If he was here, then, it was because he had reasons, however vague, to suspect the redheaded stomatologist.

He couldn't read anything in the blue eyes magnified by the spectacles' lenses. The features were as stiff as concrete, and the dentist's breath smelled of stale tobacco.

"Any man is capable of becoming a murderer if he has adequate motives."

Maigret had said this one day in answer to either Pardon or a journalist.

Now someone had tried to dishonor him, to make him lose his job overnight.

To think that it might be Mélan . . . Less than twenty-four hours after his interview with the Chief Commissioner of Police not only did Maigret still have his job, but also he turned up at the dentist's. . . .

That didn't make sense. . . . Confused thoughts . . . If . . . And if . . .

But if Mélan, since it was he Maigret was seeing at the moment, had adequate motives to set the trap in which Nicole had been instrumental, wouldn't he have adequate motives to dispose of the Superintendent in another way?

"Rinse out and spit."

Maigret obeyed as the doctor watched him, standing immobile, as impassive as ever.

"Your teeth are in perfect condition and can't have caused you any pain. . . . If you had trouble last night, if you really had spasms of pain in the right side of your jaw, it could be a symptom of sinusitis."

"Isn't there anything I can do about it?"

"That's up to your regular doctor."

To put away his instruments, he had turned his back. Maigret clambered out of the chair, which hadn't been lowered. Going a step forward, he was less than two yards from the window and, through the net curtains, he could see Aline in a negligee smoking a cigarette and looking into the street.

He knew how the rooms were arranged in the apartment opposite. The window where Manuel's mistress was standing belonged to the small room where the invalid spent the brightest moments of his day.

He paled slightly, because this discovery filled him with retrospective fear, fear that was far more definite than what he had felt the moment before.

"What do I owe you?" he muttered.

"My assistant will deal with that."

Looking as calm as ever, his motionless face just as gauche, his eyes expressionless, the doctor opened the door of the little office where Maigret had had his card filled in.

Without a word the dentist closed the door. His assistant pointed to the chair where Maigret had sat before.

"Just a minute."

She was obviously going to show in the sad-looking patient.

On the desk was a long, narrow wooden rack where cards were lying in sections like card packs in a baccarat shoe. The temptation was strong. It might have been a trap. Maigret didn't budge.

"Do you have Social Security? Can I see your card?"

He searched for it in his wallet, crammed with useless papers, and handed it to the ugly woman. She noted the number.

"It's twenty francs for the visit. . . . Your office will refund you eighty percent."

She returned his card. She wasn't wasting any charm either. She waited for him to reach the door and pressed a switch, which gave a feeble ring on the ground floor.

"You may go down."

"Thank you."

Once again he was on the staircase with its peculiar smell. The Spanish maid was waiting for him at the foot of the stairs and followed him to the door, which she shut behind him. By a miracle Lucas had been able to park in the shade and was reading a newspaper at the steering wheel.

Maigret looked up, couldn't see Aline at the window any more, and went into the building opposite.

On the third floor he rang, heard the throb of a vacuum cleaner, and the door was opened by the old maid he'd seen on former visits.

"Is it for Monsieur Palmari?"

"And Mademoiselle Aline."

"I think madam's in the bath. Come in." He was again in the sitting room. The door of the little room was open, and Manuel, in silk pajamas, was listening to the radio. He switched it off reluctantly.

"Again?"

Maigret went in, and the vacuum cleaner started to roar again on the upholstery of the sitting room.

"It's mainly Aline I want to talk to."

"She was here a few minutes ago."

"I know. I saw her at the window."

"She's gone to have a bath. . . . What did you want her for?"

"To tell the truth, I still don't know."

"Look, Superintendent . . . I've always been straight with you. . . . When you've needed it, I've done you favors, and if they'd been found out, they'd have earned me more bullets than the ones I got three years ago. . . .

"Now you're going too far, and I'm fed up with being blamed for every little thing that happens in Paris. . . . How would you like it if you were always being watched suspiciously and asked pointless questions without even being told what it's all about? . . ."

"That's just about what's happening to me at the moment, isn't it?"

"That's a good reason for not pestering other people. Aline saw you get out of the car just now and ring at the dentist's. . . . All because she told you she went there to have her teeth looked after yesterday . . ."

"No . . ."

"Then why? I can't understand any more. You're not going to tell me he's your dentist, too. . . ."

"I'm waiting for Aline. . . . So I won't have to repeat myself."

He went to the window and, his hands in his pockets, looked out and gazed at the window with net curtains behind which Dr. Mélan worked.

You couldn't see in. You could only just see lighter patches, like the dentist's smock as he approached the window to take an instrument.

"How many times have I come in a week, Manuel?"

"Three times . . . You take up such a lot of room I'd

like to say ten. . . . When I was on Rue Fontaine it didn't matter so much. . . . In a bar people come and go. . . . Everybody has the right to have a drink, and a lot of clients like to have a chat. . . . So much the worse for the owner if he's bothered. It's his job.

"But this is our own apartment, Aline's and mine. Somebody's apartment is sacred, isn't it? Not even the police can come in without a warrant. . . . Am I right?"

Maigret hadn't been listening and replied with a vague gesture.

"How many times," he asked, "have I stood at this window while I've been talking to you?"

Manuel shrugged. The question seemed idiotic.

"All I know is that you don't remain seated for long."

In his office, as on Boulevard Richard-Lenoir, Maigret used to walk to the window and stand there gazing at anything—the windows opposite, the trees, the Seine or the passers-by. Maybe it was a sign of claustrophobia? Everywhere, he instinctively sought some contact with the open air.

Aline came in wearing a bright-yellow bathrobe, drops of water in her untidy hair.

"What did I say yesterday? Did he bring his pajamas?"

But, confronted by a Maigret looking more solemn than usual, she stopped joking.

"Look, Aline, I haven't come to pester you, and I give you my word that the investigation I'm making has nothing to do with you or Manuel—anyhow, at least so far. . . ."

She scowled at him, still suspicious.

"Tell me frankly—it'll be better for everyone, believe

me—was yesterday the first time you went to the house opposite?"

"Of course. I had a toothache for the first time in my life."

"I saw you a moment ago leaning on the window sill smoking a cigarette."

"Were you there?"

She pointed to the window with the net curtains.

"In the chair you sat in. I suppose you lean on the window sill quite often?"

"Like everyone else . . . One must get some air. . . ."

"Do you know any of the people living in that house?"

"Are there many? I thought . . ."

"You thought what?"

"That there was only the doctor, Carola and the assistant."

"Is Carola the maid?"

"Maid, cook, housekeeper, anything you like . . . She's the only one who keeps the place going. . . . I occasionally meet her in the local shops. . . . Because of her accent I asked her if she was Spanish, and she said yes. She's not talkative but we say good morning to each other anyway."

"And the assistant?"

"Mademoiselle Motte."

"Did Carola tell you her name?"

"Yes. She doesn't live in the house. At twelve o'clock she has lunch in a little restaurant at the end of the street and starts work again at about two. In the evening it's less regular. . . . Sometimes she stays till seven or eight."

"Do you know where she lives?"

"I never thought about it. Close up she's even more frightening than at a distance."

"Did she fill in your card?"

"Like a passport."

"Did she ask you any prying questions?"

"She asked me who gave me the doctor's address. I said I lived opposite. In fact, she did ask me a strange question:

" 'What floor?' "

"Is that all?"

"Just about . . . I can't think . . . Unless . . . I was standing in front of her. She looked me up and down with her hard, wicked little eyes.

" 'Is there anything else the matter with you?' she asked me.

"I said no and she didn't insist. You don't take a vaccination certificate to the dentist's, do you?"

Manuel knew Maigret well enough to realize that he was getting close to a vague clue. He could feel him nosing on every side, right, left. . . . He handed Aline the photograph of Nicole Prieur.

"Have you ever seen her on Rue Fontaine?"

"Is it the young lady you told us about yesterday?"

He nodded.

"Not on Rue Fontaine . . . But I've seen her on this street, on the sidewalk opposite."

"Was she going to the dentist?"

"Exactly. Except that it was never during office hours."

"Late at night."

"Not particularly late . . . Nine, half past nine . . ."

"Was the light on in the office?"

"Not those times."

"Do you mean the light's on other evenings?"

"Quite often, yes."

"Can you see through the net curtains?"

"No. They close the shutters. Still, you can see light through the cracks."

"If I'm not mistaken, Nicole Prieur doesn't come to see Dr. Mélan as a patient."

He knew that since the evening before.

"Does the doctor see other people out of office hours? Men? . . . Women? . . ."

Aline opened her eyes wide.

"Oh! That reminds me. . . . I occasionally see men go in in the daytime, but there aren't as many men as women."

"Young?"

"There are young ones and less young ones. . . . You know, I'm not a hall porter and I don't spend my time spying on the people who go in and out. . . . I just happen to stand by the window a lot of the time."

"I've often complained about it," muttered Manuel. "I wondered if there wasn't some young man or if she wasn't getting bored with me."

"You idiot!"

"Idiot or not, I know how old I am, and this wretched leg doesn't help."

"Thousands of young men, as you say, don't come up to your ankle."

The allusion was transparent. Manuel's smile betrayed his pride, and they really looked in love with each other.

"Are there men at night, too?"

"What's going on in your head?"

"Nothing definite yet. I'm fumbling. . . ."

"It looks as though you're fumbling in odd places."

"What do you mean?"

"About these women at night. Don't you think they go for their teeth? Well, since he sees them in the office it can't be for any monkey tricks either. . . . There must be more comfortable places in the building for that sort of thing, and the doctor doesn't have a jealous woman to make scenes. . . . Do you think they've got something other than their teeth the matter with them?"

"Have you ever been pregnant?"

She looked at Manuel, who shrugged.

"Like everyone else, for Heaven's sake!"

"Have you got any children?"

"Don't talk about it! . . . The world's so badly run. . . . When you don't want any, your belly swells up just from looking at a man. . . . And then when, like now, you would like a child in the house . . . Isn't that true, Daddy? . . . Hell! There's nothing happening."

"Did a doctor help you?"

"In those days I couldn't afford a doctor. . . . The ones who do those things ask an enormous amount because of the risk. . . . So I went to a Madame Pipi."

"A ladies'-room attendant?"

"Don't tell me you don't know! There are at least ten of them in Montmartre always ready, at a small price, to help girls in a scrape."

She was staring into space; a recollection was coming to her.

"Hey! If you're right, I see why the old magpie stared at me from head to foot as though she were studying my anatomy. . . . That would also explain why she asked me if I had anything wrong with me besides my teeth."

"Did the dentist ask you anything special?"

"He hardly opened his mouth. Close up it looks as though his eyes are going to pop out of his red head. . . . 'Open' . . . 'Rinse' . . . 'Spit' . . . 'Open' . . ."

"Are you seeing him again?"

"Tomorrow morning . . . He put a temporary filling in, which has a filthy taste and ruins my cigarettes."

"If I were to ask you . . ."

But Manuel interrupted.

"None of that, Superintendent . . . We do you little favors, all right. . . . Not that that stops you from trying to implicate me . . . No use protesting . . . I know what I know. . . . But this business is like Aline's filling: it stinks! And all I have to say about it is 'No!' I even forbid her to go back to that house. Filling or no filling, she'll just have to go to another dentist."

7

At half past eleven Maigret went into his office and threw his hat on a chair. Before he had had time to select a fresh pipe there was a knock on the door and old Joseph came in.

"The Chief wants to see you, sir. . . . It's the third time he's sent for you."

In fact, sad Barnacle, with his oversensitive feet, was not the oldest member of the building—it was the usher with the silver chain, who, after spending his life in an anteroom that never saw the light of day, had turned the color of ivory.

The Superintendent followed him and, for the second time that morning, entered the Chief's office, the threshold of which he had crossed on thousands of previous occasions.

"Sit down, Maigret."

The Chief pointed to an armchair standing half in the sun and half in the shade. Through the three windows one could hear every noise from outside, and, to make the interview seem more confidential, the Chief got up to close them.

He seemed excessively embarrassed. His name was Roland Blutet. Ever since his appointment he had appeared ill at ease in his job, because at that period there were still several veterans like Maigret at the heads of the various squads.

He had tried to catch the tone of the Police Judiciare, a tone difficult to define, rough and familiar, with no unnecessary politeness, based on mutual confidence.

Not so long ago it had been a group of men most of whom did not have university degrees but who had seen almost everything there was to see on a human level. Nothing surprised them. Nothing shocked them either.

They had been faced by the most hardened criminals and had often seen them weep. They had also seen men risk their lives to arrest another criminal who would be released by the courts and begin all over again.

"I called for you three times this morning, Maigret."

"So I've just been told."

"You weren't in your office."

The Chief didn't know where to look, and his hand trembled as he lit a cigarette.

"I thought your men were giving priority to the jewel robbers and their last exploits on Avenue Victor-Hugo."

"That's right."

"It's half past eleven. . . ."

He was wearing a waistcoat, with a flat watch at the end of a chain in the pocket.

"May I ask you where you spent the morning?"

It was tougher than with the Commissioner. To start with, it was happening at the Quai des Orfèvres and not in a place that, for Maigret, was almost anonymous. He had come into this office in his shirt sleeves to chat with chiefs who had formerly been colleagues and friends.

Blutet, moreover, played his part badly.

"I went to the dentist."

"I suppose you went to one in your area?"

"Do I have to tell you, sir? Until this moment, with the exception of yesterday, I've conducted numerous interrogations, but I've never been submitted to any. I didn't realize we had to give the name and address of our dentist, doctor and possibly also our tailor. . . ."

"I see your point."

"Really?" he retorted ironically.

"I'm putting myself in your position, believe me. . . . And I don't enjoy being in mine right now. . . . I'm just obeying orders from above. . . . What would you say if I asked you to tell me how you spent your time, hour by hour, since yesterday afternoon?"

"I'd resign."

"Try to see my point . . . You're aware of the publicity the papers are giving these jewel robberies, which have succeeded each other for two months with a sort of insolence."

"Over half of them have been on the Riviera and in Deauville, outside our jurisdiction."

"But it's always the same gang! . . . At any rate, the same methods . . . The last robbery took place yesterday morning. . . . Did you go to the spot, as you usually do?"

"No."

"Have you read your detectives' reports?"

"No."

"Have you got a clue?"

"I've had the same clue ever since the robberies began again. . . ."

"With no result?"

"No, I haven't yet had any proof. . . . I'm waiting for a slip, a mistake, a little fact of no apparent importance that would permit me to act."

"This morning you did not go to your dentist but to a dentist on Rue des Acacias, and your teeth are in perfect condition. . . . Do you suspect this dentist of having any connection with the jewel robberies?"

"No."

"Your second call was at the house opposite. . . ."

"Where one of my informers lives."

"Did you discuss the jewel robberies with him?"

"No."

"Listen to me, Maigret. You know that when I came here I had the greatest admiration for you as a man and as a detective. . . . Nothing has changed. . . . Today, as I said, I have to play a part I don't enjoy. . . .

"Yesterday you were summoned by the Chief Commissioner of Police. . . . He spoke to you about a matter that has nothing to do with me and of which I know, and only need to know, the bare outline. . . . Before leaving you he especially begged you not to follow the matter up, either at close quarters or at a distance, not to mention it to anyone, not even to your colleagues and detectives. . . . Is that right?"

"That's right."

The Chief glanced at a piece of paper in front of him.

"Yesterday, then, after this interview, you stayed in

your office until about three o'clock. Then you went to a little café on Rue de Seine called Chez Désiré. Later you went to a hotel on Rue des Ecoles, where you had a brief talk with the manageress. Have these two places any connection with the matter you were forbidden to follow up?"

"Yes."

"Then you went with Inspector Janvier to Rue des Acacias, where you spent considerable time with a suspicious individual named Manuel Palmari, whom you have been known to use as an informer."

"I suppose I've been shadowed by what the papers call 'the parallel police,' sir?"

He didn't say "chief," as he used to. He was heartbroken. What's more, the sun was in his eyes and his face was covered with sweat.

Roland Blutet pretended not to hear.

"Back at the Quai you summoned an old detective named Barnacle and gave him an assignment. . . . He was to photograph a certain person without her knowing it, a person whom the Chief Commissioner of Police . . ."

". . . had forbidden me to have anything to do with . . ."

"A little later you were in a small bar on Rue Monsieur-le-Prince with Chief Inspector Lucas and a hall porter at the Sorbonne. Was that in connection with the jewel robbery?"

"No."

"With the girl I mentioned?"

"Yes."

"Was it by chance that you took Madame Maigret to dine in a restaurant on Avenue de la Grande-Armée?"

"No."

"Or that by questioning a certain Landry you managed to see the club register?"

"It's all true, sir. I admit it didn't even occur to me to see whether I was being followed. . . . Up till now I've been living on the other side of the fence. . . ."

"If it's of any interest to you, I can assure you that I've got nothing to do with these shadowings and that I only found out this morning the little I know about the matter. . . . In higher circles it seems to be of great importance. . . . I'm an official. I have to carry out the assignment I'm given."

"Do you want written confessions?"

"Don't make my job more difficult, Maigret. . . . Believe me. I'm by no means proud of it."

"I can well believe it."

"Finally, within twenty-four hours you've detached at least three detectives in your squad for jobs they weren't supposed to perform; in other words, for your personal convenience. . . . I don't suppose they will get into any trouble, because these men knew nothing about your interview with the Chief Commissioner of Police. . . . Finally . . ."

The Chief was feeling hot, too, and wiped his face.

"Finally, I have to tell you about the solution that has been suggested to me. . . . You need some rest. You've been working hard recently without taking a vacation. . . . You're to apply for sick leave, which will last until the investigation concerning you is over."

He ended with difficulty. He no longer dared look at the man sitting opposite him. He felt the embarrassment of somebody confronted by an animal he wanted to kill and only managed to wound.

"It'll probably last only a few days. According to the regulations, you'll be given time to defend yourself. . . . I believe you've already made known your version of the facts."

Maigret got up heavily.

"Thank you, sir."

Then, to the Chief's amazement, he went toward the first window.

"I suppose I can open them again?"

He opened them one by one, taking his time to breathe in the hot air from outside, to see human beings moving around in the good old Paris setting.

"Your leave begins at once. . . ."

He nodded and went out. The Chief didn't give him his hand but held it just in front of him, ready to shake the Superintendent's if he made a gesture.

Maigret didn't make it. He didn't collapse either, as he had done the day before, in the chair in his office, but made straight for the detectives' room.

"Lucas! . . . Janvier! . . ."

He didn't see Barnacle.

"Come in, boys . . . You'll be working on your own for a while. . . ."

Janvier went white and clenched his teeth, realizing he couldn't say a word.

"I'm tired, maybe I'm ill. . . . The administration, that good mother, is concerned about my health and is giving me a rest."

He walked up and down so as not to show his closest colleagues that his eyes were damp.

"You'll continue to deal with the jewel-robbery case. . . . You both know what I think about it. . . . And you know how stubborn I am. . . ."

His pipe had gone out, so he put it in the glass ashtray and filled another one.

"In higher circles they know exactly what you did yesterday. . . . They know what I did, too, of course. . . . You must warn Barnacle as soon as he comes back. . . .

"You'll probably both be followed, as I have been and as I shall continue to be. . . . On the other hand, it wouldn't do me any good if you were to get into trouble. . . . So forget all you know about the matter."

He smiled at them.

"Well! . . . That's all. . . . It was easier for me than it was for the Chief just now."

He went to the chair where he'd left his hat.

"Good-by, boys."

Janvier was the first to speak.

"You know, chief . . ."

"Yes?"

"I went to the Clou Doré. . . . I showed the photograph. . . . Nobody recognized it."

"It doesn't matter any more."

"Are you giving up?"

He looked at them in turn.

"Don't you know me any better than that?"

"Do you mean to say you'll carry on, all by yourself, with no help and your movements watched?"

"I'll try."

This time they both smiled emotionally, not knowing what to do or how to express themselves.

"Come on . . . no sentimentality . . . See you soon."

He cut the handshakes short, went to the door, and, a few minutes later, ran down the main staircase of the Police Judiciare.

When he came through the archway the two police-men on duty saluted him, and he returned their salute with a touch of irony. It was funny suddenly to see the world with another eye, the eye of a free man.

He had nothing to do, no reason to turn right rather than left.

Maybe it was one of the fishermen on the river bank who'd leave his rod and follow him. Or the chauffeur of a gray car parked a hundred yards away.

He chose to turn right. . . . It was like every other day when he went into the Brasserie Dauphine, where the owner came up to him as usual and shook his hand.

"How are you, Superintendent?"

"Fine!"

"What'll you have?"

"I wonder . . ."

He wanted a different drink, not a commonplace apéritif. He remembered his first days in Paris. A new drink was being introduced then, and it had been his favorite apéritif for one or two years.

"Does mandarin-curaçao still exist?"

"Yes. It's not much in demand, and the young people don't know what it is, but we've still got a bottle on our shelves. . . . A squirt of lemon?"

He drank two of them, but they didn't quite have the taste they used to. Then he walked slowly to Châtelet and waited for his bus. He was in no hurry.

"Are you depressed?" asked Madame Maigret, as she laid the table, because she was surprised to see her husband come back so early.

"No. It was pretty rough at the time, rougher than with the Chief Commissioner. I don't know why—

maybe because it happened in our building. . . . I feel free now, and it's quite a relief."

"Aren't you frightened?"

"All I risk is an administrative penalty, and the worst that could happen would be to retire in advance."

"I don't mean that. . . . The people who want to get you."

"They can't make another move without proving me right. This morning the Chief said a word too many. He said:

" 'Your teeth are in perfect health.'

"If it hadn't been for that, I could have thought he'd got his information from the men who were shadowing me. They didn't see inside my mouth. . . . Even our dentist, Ajoupa, couldn't state that my teeth were in good health this morning, because he hasn't seen me for over a year. . . .

"That means that after I left, Dr. Mélan must have called Nicole Prieur. . . . She complained again to her uncle. . . . The same chain as yesterday morning: Minister of the Interior, Commissioner of Police and, finally, Chief of the Police Judiciare . . . If one can be detached about it, it's quite amusing."

"What are you going to do all day?"

"Carry on."

"On your own?"

"One's never completely on one's own. . . . That reminds me! . . . I'll start off by calling good old Pardon. . . . He must have finished his rounds."

Soon after, Dr. Pardon said:

"I've just come back and I was sitting down to lunch."

"Look, Pardon, I need you once again."

He had indeed called Pardon several times for some medical detail or information about one of his colleagues.

Without knowing each other personally it's quite easy for doctors to find out about each other. Since they've all been to the same schools, they've always got a friend who studied with So and So or So and So, a professor, or a former intern in a hospital.

The circle is fairly closed and, what's more, they're always meeting at congresses.

"This time it's about a dentist, or, rather, as the nameplate says, a stomatologist."

"Personally, I don't know many of them."

"It's a certain François Mélan, age thirty-eight, who lives and works in a private house on Rue des Acacias."

There was a silence on the end of the line.

"Do you know him?"

"No . . . I was working it out. . . . It's always the problem of age. Thirty-eight, that's already another generation. . . . It'll be easier for me to find some professor who knows him."

"Could you do it fairly quickly?"

"With luck . . . I'll make a few phone calls. I might get him first go, or last go. . . . I'll have to consult my directories, too. . . . Is it important?"

"Very. For me personally . . . Have you got any plans for this evening?"

He heard him ask his wife:

"Got any plans for this evening?"

In the background he could even overhear Pardon's wife answer:

"Yesterday you suggested taking me to the movies. . . ."

"No, no plans," said Pardon on the telephone.

"How about the movies?"

"Did you hear? . . . I don't care about the movies."

"Can you both come to dinner? . . . Bring your daughter if she's still there."

"No, she's gone back to her husband."

"See you this evening, then?"

"See you this evening . . . If I hear anything earlier, I'll call you at your office."

"I haven't got an office any more."

"What? . . . Are you serious? . . ."

"Let's say that until further notice I'm just a normal citizen with no privileges and no responsibility."

It was like a Sunday afternoon, except that Paris all around him lived her weekday life, and the noises, smells and lights were not Sunday ones.

After lunch he dropped off to sleep in an armchair without realizing it, and when he opened his eyes he was astonished to see it was half past three.

"I really slept . . ." he said in a thick voice.

"You even snored. Would you like a cup of coffee?"

"I'd love one."

He needed to get his ideas straight, but he refused to think about the case and preferred to let it discharge itself inside him.

What could he do? Hardly anything. In all probability somebody on Boulevard Richard-Lenoir was on duty, waiting to follow him wherever he went.

There was no possibility of going to Boulevard de Courcelles, even less of waiting for Nicole Prieur at the

Sorbonne. She might call for help, and that would put him in a ridiculous position.

Would he be allowed to call at Dr. Mélan's door again? Unlikely. He wasn't even sure if he could go to Manuel's flat. As for calling him up, that was impossible because he himself had ordered the police to tap the telephone of the Clou Doré's proprietor.

"I put some sugar in. . . . Careful; it's very hot."

She looked at her husband with slight anxiety, and he smiled at her good-humoredly.

"Don't worry, Madame Maigret. . . . Your old husband will survive. . . ."

It was when he was in high spirits that he called her "Madame Maigret," and she was surprised.

"You look calm."

"I am."

"You don't look as though you had any problems."

"That's because they're bound to solve themselves."

"Are you going out?"

"I'm going for a short walk."

"Are you sure there's no danger?"

"A bus or a car, as usual . . ."

Nevertheless, he did just betray his latent excitement. He drank his coffee in little sips.

"Did you do the shopping for dinner?"

"I called up. . . . It's all been delivered. . . . Do you want to know what we're eating?"

"I'd rather have a surprise."

He hadn't gone a hundred yards in the street before he turned around and saw the men shadowing him. There were two of them, and they suddenly tried to gesticulate as though they were having a violent argument.

Maigret didn't know them. They must belong to a branch directly connected with the Ministry of the Interior.

Like that, he went as far as the Bastille. He thought of shaking the two men off, just to play them a trick, but gave up the idea and shrugged his shoulders.

He sat for nearly an hour outside a café like a man of means, reading the evening papers he'd just bought at a stand.

He went home along Boulevard Beaumarchais and Rue du Chemin-Vert. Since he had time to spare, he had a shower and dressed.

Pardon hadn't telephoned. The couple arrived at eight, and they sat down to dinner at once, since there was a soufflé as first course, followed by coq au vin.

"It took me some time, but I finally got hold of somebody who knows your man very well. . . . I'll tell you about it later."

"Do you remember what we said last time we dined with you? The vicious criminal . . . Evil for evil's sake . . . I replied that I had no reason to believe in it. . . . This evening I think I may be mistaken. . . ."

He didn't want to say any more about it at the table. The coffee was served in the drawing room, and the two men took theirs into the little study Maigret had fitted up for himself.

"Please excuse us, ladies."

"Would you like some prunelle or framboise?"

Pardon replied for both of them:

"Neither."

The window was open and, just as during their last conversation, night was falling. The only difference was that the air was calm, the sky clear, with no threat of a storm.

"It was only after my fifth or sixth telephone call that one of my colleagues reminded me of a man I used to know quite well at one time, and whose sister I knew even better. I believe that when I was about eighteen I vaguely intended to marry her. . . .

"I'd lost touch with both of them. . . . It so happens that this man Vivier lives almost next door to me on Boulevard Voltaire. . . . I looked in on him between visits. . . . He's a professor of stomatology and knows François Mélan very well; he calls him 'young Mélan' and had him as a pupil. . . ."

Pardon gave Maigret a long look before asking him:

"Are you very interested in him? . . . Is it a criminal case? . . ."

And the Superintendent answered slowly:

"If I'm wrong, I'll retire in a week to Meung-sur-Loire, but if I'm right, this is the strangest case of my career."

"Does the case center around Mélan?"

"Yes."

"That's odd."

"Why?"

"Because there are certain similarities between what you've just said and Vivier's opinion. Have you seen Mélan?"

"This morning, under pretext of a toothache."

"Is he tall, short-sighted, with red hair, blue eyes and long arms?"

"I didn't notice the length of his arms."

"What did he say to you?"

"That my teeth were in good condition."

"The first thing to know about him is that he comes from a very poor and humble family. His father was a day laborer in a village on the Somme. . . . The family was just about the most wretched one there, and to make matters worse the father got drunk every Saturday. He had five children. François Mélan had, and must still have, a sister two or three years older than he. . . Vivier found all this out only after having known his pupil a long time.

"For two years he hardly knew anything about him. Mélan isn't a man who takes people into his confidence. He had no friends. He was supposed not to be having any love affairs. . . .

"At the College they didn't realize that he worked all night to pay for his studies, and Vivier still wonders where he did his secondary schooling and in what conditions. I'll try to quote a few of the things he said:

" 'A talented boy of brilliant intelligence, with a secretive, tortured character . . .' "

Maigret listened as though he were classifying each word in his brain.

"Vivier ended up by taking him as his assistant, both to do him a favor and because he was the best of his pupils.

" 'To start with it depressed me,' he admitted to me. 'It's upsetting to have an assistant who doesn't say a word out of work and whose private life is a mystery. . . . One evening I invited him to dinner and I had to force him to confide in me. . . . After dinner I took him into my office and tried to get him to talk about himself. . . . We drank some wine. I served some brandy. . . . He drank it reluctantly. . . . Little by little, however, he came to life, and I discovered fragments of his past. . . .' "

Pardon lit a cigar and looked at Maigret again.

"Does that still seem in character?"

"I can't wait to hear the rest of it."

"It's simple and dramatic. . . . At the College, Mélan's comrades nicknamed him 'the Virgin.' There was even a rumor that he had homosexual tendencies. . . .

"The story he told Vivier accounts for his behavior. If I'm not mistaken, he was fourteen during the German invasion. His family was too poor to escape along the roads with many of the others. . . .

"One evening Mélan and his sister were standing by the side of the road when two motorcyclists appeared. . . . They were the first German soldiers they had ever seen. They stopped to ask them where some village was. Then they started speaking to each other and laughing. . . .

"Finally they signaled to the girl to lie down on the embankment, and when she hesitated they pulled her down. . . . They both raped her before they left and laughed at the boy, who hadn't moved. . . .

"The revelation of the sexual act in these conditions might well have had a traumatic effect on a sensitive child. . . .

" 'Is this why you're never seen around with girls?' asked Vivier.

"And his assistant replied awkwardly:

" 'I don't know. . . . Maybe one day I'll get married like everybody else. . . . I don't know if I'd dare, if I could ever make a woman happy. . . .' "

There was a silence. Maigret looked so solemn that Pardon was the first to speak.

"Do you think he's committed a crime?"

The Superintendent didn't answer at once.

"Until now I didn't envisage a real crime. But now I'm almost certain of it. . . . Did the professor say anything else to you?"

"Not about Mélan. About his assistant, who's also worked for Vivier . . . Did you see her, too?"

"Yes."

"Is it true she's so ugly?"

"Worse than that."

"People say she's a shrew—that was the word Vivier used. In fact, she's the most sensitive and dedicated girl in her quarter; she's the one who always gets waked up when there's an invalid to be looked after or somebody dying in the neighborhood. . . ."

"Which is her quarter?"

"I didn't ask. I can ring Vivier and ask for her address."

8

Maigret was extraordinarily serene. None of his thoughts appeared on the surface—he had simply acquired an added depth. For the first time Pardon was seeing him at the moment when the various strings of an investigation were beginning to tie up, when something true was gradually taking shape, and he watched his friend as though he were trying to discover the mechanism at work behind that heavy expressionless face.

"What sort of a man is Vivier? Is he broad-minded?"

"Except about state intervention in medicine. He's one of the most violent protesters, a rabid individualist!"

Puffing slowly on his pipe the Superintendent fell silent again, but without looking as though he were pondering. He looked slightly absent, and it was a surprise to see him return to the exact point in the conversation where he had left off.

"Is there any chance of finding him at home?"

"He's preparing a vast treatise on stomatology, which will be his life's work, and he spends part of the night at it."

"Would you call him up and ask him if I could have a few words with him?"

The next minute the doctor had Vivier on the line.

"This is Pardon. . . . I'm calling you from my friend Maigret's house and I apologize for disturbing you at work. . . . The Superintendent would like to talk to you."

The answer must have been funny, because the doctor smiled.

"Yes . . . Here he is. . . ."

He handed Maigret the receiver.

"I apologize, too, professor. . . . If you could answer two or three questions, you'd facilitate my task enormously. . . . Yes, Pardon has told me about your conversation, which is of vital interest to me. . . .

"I'd like to mention that I'm appealing to you in a private capacity. . . . I'm on sick leave for an indefinite period of time. . . . No, I'm not ill, or, if I am, it's very serious, because my friend Pardon, who's my regular doctor, says I'm in perfect health. . . .

"The truth is that during an investigation I've had to deal with some powerful people, and since I'm in the habit of finishing what I've started I've been told to rest for a few days. . . .

"This is my first question, professor: would you be very surprised to hear that your former assistant, Dr. Mélan, has committed one or more crimes?"

At the other end of the line there was a sort of bark that could be taken for a laugh. When Vivier's voice could be heard, it was the sonorous voice of a man who has his own opinions and expresses them with vigor.

"My dear Superintendent, I'd hardly be amazed if I were to hear the same thing about me, you or my porter. . . . Under sufficient external or internal pressure, anyone is capable of committing acts which the law and morality would frown at. . . ."

"In his case would you think it more likely to be internal or external pressure?"

"Have you met him?"

"This morning, for a few minutes."

"Did Pardon tell you what I thought of Mélan?"

"He's just done so."

"What's your opinion?"

"I'd rather know yours."

"Internal pressure, undoubtedly! Mélan is the typical introvert who never lets his emotions appear on the surface. Apart from one or two conversations, when I managed, not without difficulty, to persuade him to talk about himself, he's probably never confided in anyone."

"Supposing he had committed a crime, any crime, would you admit the possibility of extenuating circumstances?"

"Are you asking me as a doctor or as a man? As a doctor it isn't my field. I'd leave it to the psychiatrists to decide, and their opinion would depend on the circumstances."

He added ironically:

"On the age of the psychiatrists, too, and the school they belong to."

"And as a man?"

"Personally, knowing him as well as I do, I'd willingly be a witness for the defense."

"My second question is harder to ask and I'm afraid it will surprise you. . . . Would a man like Mélan, who feels himself trapped, act in a simple or a complicated way?"

"Monsieur Maigret, you seem to know him almost as well as I do. . . . In a complicated way, of course! . . . And the word 'complicated' isn't strong enough. When he worked with me, Mélan always chose the most complicated way, even to reply to an examination question. . . . His is the complete opposite to what I'd call a one-way brain. . . . He takes all the possibilities, all the possible ramifications of a subject into account and tries not to leave anything in the dark."

"Thank you . . . I have one more favor to ask you, if you think you can grant it and trust me . . . I might be wrong, and the theories that I'm formulating at the moment might prove false before the night is over. . . . On the other hand, if the facts confirm them, several people are running a serious risk. . . . A conversation with Mademoiselle Motte would undoubtedly clear up this point. . . .

"I suppose she's got a telephone. . . . If you could arrange for her to see me either at her house or anywhere else this evening, it might avoid new complications."

"Does poor Motte frighten you, too? When I think that without her ugly face everyone would think her an angel! . . . I'll call her up. . . . Where can I call you back? . . ."

Maigret got up and went into the sitting room, where

131

the two women were talking in a whisper so as not to disturb them.

"I'd love a drop of prunelle. . . . Unless Pardon takes the glass out of my hand . . ."

Pardon didn't do a thing. He went on watching his friend with admiring curiosity tinged with fear.

He wondered on what basis Maigret had formulated his theories and he would have liked to reconstruct his train of thought.

"Hello . . . Yes, it's me, professor. . . . She's prepared to see me right away? . . . It wasn't too difficult? . . . Rather? . . . May I ask you her address? . . . Rue des Francs-Bourgeois, yes . . . Yes . . . Yes . . . I know the building. . . . I lived near there for some time, in Place des Vosges. . . . I'm very grateful to you. . . . Yes . . . I'd like to meet you, too. . . ."

When he got up he was just as serene, but in his eyes was a gleam that hadn't been there before.

"You won't be angry with me, will you, Pardon, if I leave you with these ladies? . . . There is actually a chance that my phone's being tapped. . . . I wonder if some people interested in my affairs won't be there before me. . . . In the street there must be one or two special detectives going the rounds."

"Why don't I drive you there? I've got my car. I'll be back in a few minutes."

They went into the sitting room.

"Are you going out? For long?"

"I've no idea when I'll be back."

"Are you running any risk?"

"Not at this stage . . . Pardon's dropping me and is coming right back."

On the way he didn't say a word. No car followed

him. Knowing he was with Pardon, had they relaxed their attention?

Rue des Francs-Bourgeois, in the Marais district, still had a few historic houses, which now sheltered a crowd of needy families, mainly small artisans, many of them from Poland, Hungary, or Lithuania.

"Good night, Pardon . . . Thanks . . . If I succeed it'll be largely owing to you."

"Good luck."

Maigret rang. The invisible porter released the latch of a little side door stuck in the gateway, and he crossed what had once been the main courtyard of some great nobleman.

"Mademoiselle Motte, please?"

From a dormer window a voice replied:

"The second on the left . . . First door . . ."

The lights on the stairway went on the minute he went up them, and he saw Dr. Mélan's assistant bending over the banisters. When he got up to her floor, she murmured:

"I thought you wouldn't find your way. . . . The house is quite complicated. . . ."

She looked different in a dark dress from when she wore a uniform, more vulnerable, one might have said. Her anxiety was evident in her deep-set eyes. On her pale skin there were red patches brought on by worry.

"This way . . . Hurry up . . . The lights will go off."

She showed him into a very clean, almost gay room, used as both a sitting room and a dining room, where provincial furniture, mellowed by time, introduced a peaceful and reassuring note.

"Sit down . . . You may smoke."

"I hope the professor didn't wake you up?"

"I don't sleep much."

There was no radio or television, but masses of books on the shelves and an open one near the armchair.

"Did you leave your pipe behind?"

She didn't try to put on a welcoming smile or to conceal her anxiety.

"When I saw you this morning in the waiting room, I realized there was going to be trouble. . . . What surprises me is that you should come here."

"As I told Professor Vivier, Mademoiselle Motte, I'm here in a private capacity. . . . I have no right to bother you. . . . My superior officers have sent me on sick leave so as to avoid annoying some influential people. . . .

"You have the right to shut the door in my face, which is why I asked Professor Vivier, whom you trust, to intervene. . . . Even now you have the right not to answer my questions. . . ."

He spoke slowly and quietly, as though he were unsure of himself.

"The day before yesterday I was the target of an elaborate plot, a trap subtle enough for me almost inevitably to be caught. . . ."

Just two days! All the incidents that had happened since were confused in Maigret's mind, the important ones and the less important ones, Manuel's little wheelchair and the stains on the walls of the house opposite, the black hair of the doctor's maid and the doctor's blue eyes, enormously enlarged by his spectacles, a few inches away from the Superintendent's face . . .

Every detail would fall into place at a given moment,

together with its significance and importance in the whole.

"There's only one truth," Maigret used to maintain. "The problem is to recognize it, to get at it. . . ."

"Do you want a cup of coffee?"

"No, thanks . . . You're eager to know exactly why I came. . . . I now know enough about Dr. Mélan's past to be able to account for his behavior. . . ."

She looked at him even more attentively than Pardon some moments before, her hands folded in her lap.

"The person who set the trap for me was cornered. . . . He tends, when faced with a problem, to select the most subtle and complicated solution. . . .

"Curiously enough it took an almost miraculous coincidence of events for me to take an interest in his acts and movements. . . ."

Her eyes wide open, she muttered in amazement:

"You mean you haven't been having the doctor watched for several weeks?"

"No, Mademoiselle Motte . . . I was having a criminal who lives in the building opposite watched, and the men you saw in the street were supposed to find out who visited him and to follow his mistress when she went out."

"I can't . . ."

". . . believe me. And yet it's true. I myself have recently been several times to see this man, named Manuel Palmari, and, according to an old habit, I occasionally stood by the window. . . ."

"So you weren't there because of . . ."

"Because of Dr. Mélan? I didn't even know his name, and if I seemed to take an interest in his house, it's because I like old buildings. . . .

135

"I have been, as I told you, the victim of an intrigue. . . . Someone was trying to get rid of me. . . . Someone who, instead of using violence, worked out a complicated, almost diabolical plan, without a single flaw . . .

"Suspecting Manuel of certain crimes, and having had my eye on him for a long time, I started thinking it might be he and paid him several visits. . . .

"I discovered elsewhere that Mademoiselle Prieur, who played an important part in the matter, belonged to a club on Avenue de la Grande-Armée. . . . On the club register I found the name of your boss as the girl's backer, and I had a strong desire to have a closer look at him. . . ."

"It's unbelievable. . . ."

She wasn't questioning what he said, but she was astounded by the unpredictability of destiny.

"Dr. Mélan could have played the game, taken out or filled a tooth that didn't need it. . . . No, he told me honestly that my teeth were in good condition, and showed me to the door without a word or a question."

"He was terrified. . . . For several weeks he's been living in continual panic."

"Did he mention it to you?"

"No, but I know him well enough to realize it. So did Carola."

"The maid? Is she his mistress?"

"She isn't his mistress. . . . Carola sleeps at the other end of the house, in the attic, although there are so many rooms they don't know what to do with them."

"Do you understand why I'm here, Mademoiselle Motte?"

"To question me."

"Not exactly, because I don't even know which questions to ask you. I wanted to play fair with you. As I told you, I'm powerless at the moment. I'm by no means certain either, and my theories remain pretty vague. . . .

"Nobody could have contrived the intrigue of which I was the object without a major interest, unless he hated me personally. . . .

"Now, Dr. Mélan might know my game, but he never met me until this morning. . . .

"And yet my presence in the apartment opposite, after seeing my detectives in the street, terrified him. . . . Why and what powerful enough interest could he have in disarming me?

"That's where I started. What could I discover about him that would be important enough to account for his behavior?

"Here again chance played its part. Aline, Manuel's mistress, had a toothache for the first time in her life and, of course, she went to the dentist opposite.

"She may not be intelligent but she has an uncommonly good sense of intuition. She's a woman in every sense of the word.

"Mélan asked her two questions too many, or, rather, I seem to remember it was you who asked her the first:

" 'Who sent you here?'

"It's a question that a dentist or his assistant doesn't usually ask a patient.

"The second:

" 'Is there anything else the matter with you?'

"Struck by the atmosphere in the building, Aline let her imagination work. She remembered the light in the evening she frequently saw on in the office. When I asked her, she replied that after dark no men, but only women, rang at the door. . . ."

"I'm not there in the evening."

"I know. But you must know about these visits? . . ."

"Look, Superintendent. I was prepared to see you because of Professor Vivier. Nevertheless, I must tell you that I'll do anything to defend Dr. Mélan. . . . He's a man who's suffered all his life, who is now suffering more than ever, who will always suffer. . . . He had a particularly unpleasant childhood."

"I know which incident you're hinting at."

"An incident? He didn't mention any incident to me. . . . He doesn't confide in anyone."

"His sister, at the beginning of the war . . ."

"I didn't know he had a sister."

Maigret told her about the rape, and she again opened her eyes in amazement.

"That accounts for a lot. . . ."

"I can tell you that whatever happens, according to Professor Vivier, the psychiatrists will find extenuating circumstances. . . . Vivier has applied in advance as witness for the defense. . . . And I may be next to him."

"You?"

"Me. But I need your help. You agree he lives in terror. A large proportion of crimes are committed in terror. . . ."

"He'll go to prison just the same. . . . And he's not the sort of man who can stand prison."

"Everybody I've arrested has said that. . . . You know as well as I do that the doctor performed abortions, don't you?"

"I realized it one day when I found a probe, and

other objects a dentist wouldn't need, in a drawer. . . ."

"Any other evidence?"

"I can't destroy him. . . ."

"Do you want my opinion, Mademoiselle Motte? . . . First tell me if Mélan is a Christian."

"He doesn't practice any religion."

"In that case, for him, abortion isn't necessarily a serious crime. It's a question of morals, and it varies according to latitudes and countries. Some people allow it and others condemn it. You see, if that were the only thing, I don't think your boss would be so insane as to behave as he has been for the last few days. . . . Didn't this idea occur to you?"

"Yes . . ."

"Why?"

She turned away, and after a fairly long silence muttered:

"What you're asking me is terrible. . . . I'm all he has. . . ."

"What do you mean?"

"That he's always been alone . . . completely alone. . . . I know he goes out, and goes to the club you mentioned. . . . It's to reassure himself. Maybe also to . . ."

"To solicit clients?"

"I thought about that."

"And Nicole Prieur?"

"The first time, I suspected she'd come for the same reason as the others."

"As the other evening visitors?"

"Yes . . . I haven't got a card in her name. . . . She's a hysterical little girl who threw herself at him, and I'm sure she's pursuing him. . . ."

"Is she his mistress?"

There was another silence.

"Do you want me to answer for you?" suggested Maigret. "You're convinced that Mélan has never had a mistress, no more now than when he was a student and his comrades called him the Virgin. . . ."

"I didn't know about that nickname."

"Am I right?"

"That occurred to me."

"So, like me, you suspected something else. . . ."

She got up, at the end of her tether, and paced the room.

"You're torturing me."

"Would you rather there were some more crimes?"

She suddenly looked him in the eyes, distraught.

"How did you find all that out? Did Carola talk?"

"Does Carola know?"

"All right! I'll have to go through with it. I can't keep this secret any longer. I was surprised, when I started working for Dr. Mélan, to see that he always kept me out of his office when he saw a female patient. . . ."

"Do you mean the patients during the day?"

"Of course, since I wasn't there at night."

"Any female patient?"

"No. For some of them, just as I did for the men, I performed the normal functions of an assistant, handing the doctor the instruments he needed, getting the X-rays ready and so on."

"But when some female patients came you were sent to your office?"

"Yes."

"With no explanation?"

"Dr. Mélan never gives explanations."

"Did you suspect anything?"

"Because of an article in the papers . . . In the United States, in Connecticut, I believe, a dentist used to anesthetize his patients by force when they seemed attractive. . . ."

"He was probably shy, too, don't you think? Without a wife or a mistress . . ."

"Yes . . ."

"Did something happen recently to confirm your suspicions?"

"A patient came in and didn't go out. . . . I was surprised, because they always come through my office. . . . He said he'd shown her out down the back stairs. . . ."

"Did Carola say he didn't?"

"Yes. Her kitchen looks onto those stairs, and the door is always open. . . . What's more . . ."

"Go on . . ."

"Nothing . . . I can't. . . ."

"I'll help you again. . . . Does the doctor have a gardener?"

"No."

"He does the gardening himself?"

"Very little. There are more weeds than flowers."

"Did you ask Carola if, that night . . ."

"No . . . She told me."

"And you didn't mention it to anyone?"

"No . . . He's alone. . . . He thinks he's ugly. . . ."

She was alone. She was ugly.

"Is that the only accident?"

"As far as I know . . ."

"But you're not there when he sees his evening visitors. . . . Is Carola in the house?"

"Sometimes she goes to the movies."

"So there might have been other accidents. . . ."

"It's not impossible."

"Could there be any more?"

"What do you want me to do?"

"To help me. I have no right to go to Rue des Acacias, where the police could stop me. What's more, if I went, Mélan might blow his brains out. Has he got a gun?"

"Yes . . . An old army revolver."

"You must call him and say you've got something serious and urgent to tell him which it's better not to talk about on the telephone. . . . Ask him to come here. . . . I suppose he's got a car. . . . He trusts you."

"And if he brings his revolver?"

"Not to come to see you . . ."

"So he's got nobody left, not even me. . . ."

"Think of the girl, or girls, whose remains will probably be found in the garden."

"I see. . . . But it's hard just the same. . . . Why does it have to be me? . . . If you're a Catholic, it reminds you of something, doesn't it?"

And, since he shook his head, she said:

"Judas!"

Slowly she went to the telephone. Her thin fingers moved the dial. The red patches had disappeared from her face, and she kept her eyes half closed.

"Is that you, doctor? . . . This is Motte. . . ."

After she'd hung up she didn't say another word. Nor did Maigret. They sat opposite one another without looking at each other, and they waited. Twice the Superintendent lit his pipe, because he'd forgotten to pull on it.

Willpower prevented them from pacing up and down the room to still their impatience.

From time to time Maigret looked at his watch. Mademoiselle Motte could see the time above the detective's head, on the clock he could hear ticking.

It seemed a long time. Would Mélan come? If he'd understood it was all over, he might already have blown his brains out. But Carola would doubtless have heard the noise and her first reaction would have been to telephone the nurse before calling the police, whom she didn't appear to like.

Carola may have gone to the movies. And if that night Nicole Prieur . . . ? Mademoiselle Motte must have been asking herself more or less the same questions. Through the open window they could hear occasional noises from the street, the noise of a car, a passer-by, farther and farther off, a couple whose voices could be heard. . . .

It seemed an eternity, whereas in reality it was only about twenty minutes, twenty minutes of silence and immobility.

A car stopped. . . . A slight grating of brakes . . . Steps on the sidewalk, then a distant muffled ring. The door shutting in the gateway. Steps on the rugged cobbles of the courtyard, the glass door opening, the stairs . . .

Mademoiselle Motte raised her hand to her breast and muttered to herself:

"I can't. . . ."

He thought, when she stood up, that she was going to rush into the kitchen, to hide, maybe to escape down another staircase. She stood motionless, and he stood up, too, just as upset as she.

The silence was so intense that they heard the slight click of the staircase switch in the hallway. The light had gone off. A hand groped at the door, and the nurse walked three paces to open it.

Mélan wore a gray suit and held his hat in his hand. He came a yard forward, turned around without having seen Maigret, opened his mouth, then looked around and saw the Superintendent.

He didn't speak at once. Nor did he try to rush out. In spite of his surprise, and emotion, one felt that he was trying to understand, that his brain was working quickly.

The problem must have seemed difficult to solve. After a moment he shook his head, as he would have rubbed an equation off the blackboard to start again at zero. All his senses were strained to the utmost.

Now he looked at them, one after the other, his brow furrowed; then he looked at the armchairs in which they'd just been sitting, at the pipe in the ashtray, within reach of the Superintendent.

"Have you been here long?" he finally asked almost calmly.

"Quite long . . ."

His blue eyes lingered on the pained face of Motte. They expressed neither anger nor indignation. Surprise, certainly, but still, and always, a question . . . a question . . . a question . . .

He needed to understand. . . . He wanted to understand. . . . He had an exceptional brain. He'd always been told he had an exceptional brain. He'd proved it. . . . He'd started from the bottom . . . from the bottom . . . and he . . .

"It's not her fault, doctor," said Maigret, to put an

end to this painful scene. "When I came in, I already knew everything, or almost everything. I only needed confirmation. . . ."

There was no hatred in Mélan's eyes as he stared at the Superintendent. What had Pardon asked him during their last dinner on Rue Popincourt? A vicious crime, perpetrated consciously . . . Evil for evil's sake . . .

For a moment Maigret thought he'd come across it for the first time in his career. . . .

Mélan didn't hate him. Mélan didn't hate anyone. He was afraid. Maybe he'd been afraid all his life. . . .

"I telephoned Professor Vivier . . ."

The dentist's astonishment increased, but he didn't say a word; only his eyes expressed it through the enlargement of his spectacles.

"He'll be a witness for the defense. . . . I may be, too. . . ."

EPILOGUE

Twenty minutes later Mélan's car drew up in front of the police station of the Third Arrondissement on Rue Perrée, and Maigret got out first.

When they entered the hallway, it was the dentist's turn to go first.

"Farther on . . . The second door on the left . . ."

One of the detectives, his feet on the table, was reading a newspaper as he smoked his pipe; another was typing out a report on a rickety typewriter.

They both got up when they recognized the Superintendent.

"Good evening, gentlemen . . . Forgive me for disturbing you . . . I'm not on duty. I'm simply accompanying Dr. Mélan, who wants to make a statement. . . . I suppose you'll be typing it, Bassin?"

He had known him for twenty years.

"Once the document has been signed you may have to take the doctor to the Central Police Station. . . . Gently . . . No brutality . . . Good evening, doctor. . . ."

When Maigret got home, the Pardons had left. Madame Maigret hadn't gone to bed.

"Well?"

"He's confessing."

"What?"

"Everything. Everything that's on his mind . . We'll read about it tomorrow in the papers . . . the evening ones, because it's too late for the morning papers."

"Was he the one who caused the trouble?"

"He was afraid because he'd seen me at a window and thought I was watching him."

"What are you going to do?"

"Wait . . ."

The summons was brought at ten in the morning by a police cyclist. He wasn't summoned by the Chief Commissioner of Police, but by the Chief of the Police Judiciaire.

"Come in . . ."

He pushed the door open, his pipe in his mouth, as he had for years come into this office every morning, whoever the successive occupants were.

"So it's you, Maigret. . . . Sit down . . . What can I say to you?"

"Nothing, sir."

"Sir?"

"Chief, if you'd rather . . ."

"I'd rather. . . ."

"Are you angry with me?"

"No . . ."

"I called the Chief Commissioner, who called the Minister of the Interior . . ."

"Who, in turn, called his friend Jean-Baptiste Prieur. . . ."

"Probably . . . Janvier's waiting for you in your office. . . . He was on duty last night. . . . It was he who was alerted by the Third Arrondissement.

"He went this morning early with a digger to Rue des Acacias, where the remains of three women were discovered. . . .

"The first was buried about five years ago. . . . As for the second, the medical expert can't decide whether it was two or three years ago. . . . The third died less than a month ago. . . ."

The Chief also asked himself a question. "How did Maigret . . . ?"

But he didn't dare say it aloud.

"It's up to you to continue the investigation, of course. . . ."

And then to prove that Manuel was the man behind the jewel robberies.

He'd be making many more visits to Rue des Acacias.

Epalinges
July 28, 1964